"Where the hell were you?" Barry shouted. "How could you leave me locked up in here all night? What's the matter with you? You jerk! Say something!"

"But I didn't, Barry," I said. "I just went out and the door slammed, that's all. I was only gone for a second. Why won't you believe me?"

"Believe you?" He gestured around the room. "It took me hours to clean this place up." He looked down at his half-naked body, and the pile of clothes. "I finally went to sleep."

He reached up to touch his face. It was covered in pale stubble. I realized then that Barry wasn't making up what had happened to him.

"You left me in there today, for less than a minute," he said slowly. "But to me it was..." He actually began to smile. "Harry, does this mean what I think it does?"

I nodded. "Time goes faster in there," I said.

Other Bantam Starfire Books you will enjoy

SINGULARITY

William Sleator

BANTAM BOOKS
NEW YORK · TORONTO · LONDON · SYDNEY · AUCKLAND

RL 6, IL age 12 and up

*This edition contains the complete text
of the original hardcover edition.*
NOT ONE WORD HAS BEEN OMITTED.

SINGULARITY

*A Bantam Spectra Book / published by arrangement with
E. P. Dutton, Inc.*

PRINTING HISTORY

E. P. Dutton edition published April 1985
A Selection of the Junior Literary Guild, August 1985
Bantam edition / May 1986

ISBN 0-553-25627-0

Published simultaneously in the United States and Canada

Bantam Books are published by Bantam Books, a division of Bantam Double-
day Dell Publishing Group, Inc. Its trademark, consisting of the words
"Bantam Books" and the portrayal of a rooster, is Registered in U.S. Patent
and Trademark Office and in other countries. Marca Registrada. Bantam
Books, 666 Fifth Avenue, New York, New York 10103.

This book is dedicated to my sister, Vicky S. Wald. We were never actually twins—though people sometimes thought we were—but we are just as important to each other as any twins I ever heard of.

1

It was my twin brother, Barry, who wanted to go to the house—and Barry knew how to get what he wanted.

It all started with a letter from a lawyer in a place called Sushan, Illinois. An uncle of Mom's had died. She had inherited his house.

Our family was reasonably well-off, but Mom and Dad were still excited about this windfall. What the inherited house meant, basically, was the money they would make from selling it. There was never any question of giving up our own home in a suburb of Boston.

"You've never said much about this generous Uncle Ambrose of yours," Dad said.

"I must have been about ten the last time I saw him," said Mom. "The thing I remember most about him is his glass eye. It had such a peculiar fixed stare, while the real one rolled and jerked around like a bird's. I asked him to take out the glass eye. He eagerly obliged."

"Spend much time at this house?"

"Never saw the place. He didn't have much to do with the family."

"Well get this lawyer to put it on the market right away."

But it wasn't going to be that simple. The next envelope from Sushan was a large manila one. In it was a letter, explaining that the house contained a good deal of furniture, much of which might be quite valuable, as well as personal papers and books. The lawyer felt that it would be in Mom's best interests to deal with these items herself. Furthermore, he added, if the house was left in its present unoccupied state for much longer, there would be the problem of vandalism.

The envelope also contained a set of keys.

"Well, I certainly can't go until we come back from California," Mom said, irritably jangling the keys. They were leaving in three days for a convention of Dad's in San Francisco, and after that they had made plans to travel along the Pacific coast. They would be away for two weeks. Barry and I weren't going. That had been fine with us, at first. We had never been left at home on our own before.

But then Mom had begun organizing certain friends and neighbors to feed us and check up on us and supervise our activities to be sure we didn't get into any trouble. By the time she got through phoning and scheduling and writing things down on her calendar, it looked as though there would hardly be a day that we'd be left on our own. She also made a long list of Do's and Don't's—mostly Don't's, such as, Don't have any parties.

2

That part bothered Barry more than me—he was more popular than I was. But we were both dismayed when we realized that we were going to be more restricted than when Mom and Dad were around. Barry kept reminding Mom that we were sixteen and practically adults. "I mean, we shave every day now," he pointed out. "Doesn't that mean something?"

"It doesn't mean I trust you to stay here unsupervised, with all the kids in the neighborhood looking for a place to hang out," she said. Barry begged and pleaded and sulked, and even threw a couple of tantrums. But Mom remained implacable.

Now, three days before their departure, Mom shook the keys on the old, greenish metal chain and sighed. "We can't change our California plans now," she said. "We've already made all the reservations and *paid* for everything."

"So you can go to this Sushan place when we come back from California," Dad said.

"I bet it's just a crummy mobile home in the middle of a cornfield," Barry said. The closer we got to their trip, the more bitter he became. It was going to be a miserable couple of weeks.

"No, it's a big lonely old house in the country, I know that much," Mom said. "My mother said it was the most uncomfortable place she'd ever stayed in, and wouldn't go back there after I was born. And he gave it to me." She laughed and shook her head. Then she set down the keys without looking at them. "The story was Uncle Ambrose made a lot of money on the stock market. Then he lost it in the crash. Millions he lost, overnight."

3

Barry picked up the keys. He didn't look at me or change his expression, but at that moment I knew what he was thinking. Barry and I could sometimes figure out what was going on in one another's minds. At one time it gave us a lot of pleasure—we used to make a game of it and could startle other people. But in the last couple of years our special communication had begun to irritate Barry. I had learned to keep my mouth shut about it. Just as I had kept my mouth shut, a year ago, when he had told Mom we didn't want to dress alike anymore.

"Well, if he was so rich once, there probably *is* a lot of valuable stuff there—maybe even hidden money, who knows?" Barry said. "He could have been one of those crazy old people who dresses in garbage bags and lives on cat food, and then dies and they find a million one-dollar bills hidden in the mattress." He ran a finger carefully over the edge of one of the keys. "And if the house stays empty much longer, bums will start going in and camping out there, and going through stuff. *Our* stuff. And then we can just say good-bye to all the money and treasure he hoarded there for his whole life."

"You're letting your imagination run away with you, Barry," Dad said. "I'll bet the only things this Uncle Ambrose hoarded were *National Geographics.*"

"But he *was* rich once," Barry argued. "It's very likely that he did save some stuff from that time. People pay a lot of money for old furniture, don't they? And how about silverware? Maybe even jewelry and stuff. And now it's ours—I mean, Mom's. It's just plain dumb to sit here and let other people walk off with it."

Mom was really getting worried now. "There must be some family heirlooms there," she said. "They belong in the family. I'd just never forgive myself if we let them slip"—she clenched her fists—"but I've been looking forward to this trip to California so much! I don't even want to miss one day!" She sighed again. "But I suppose it's my duty."

"I bet one old oriental rug—that somebody might be stealing from the house right now—would more than pay for two tickets from Boston to Sushan," Barry said.

"So that's what you're driving at," said Dad.

"You two boys going to that house by yourselves?" Mom said.

"I'm not sure I—" I started to say.

"What's the matter? Are you scared?" Barry accused me.

"No!" I couldn't admit that I really was apprehensive. Barry would think I was siding with Mom and Dad against him. "I was just going to say—what about Fred?"

"He'll love it. He can play outside all day." Barry turned eagerly to Mom. "We couldn't get into trouble there. It's not like here, where we know hordes of wild teenagers looking for places to party, as you keep pointing out. We don't know anybody there. Anyway, they're probably all too tired from picking corn all day to stay out after eight o'clock."

"But you two don't know anything about antiques,

5

or about family papers or anything like that," said
Mom.

"You could do all that stuff later," said Barry. "We'd
just be there as caretakers, occupying the house to
keep anybody else out. Well, Harry?" he urged me,
smiling his warmest smile. "You want to go too, I can
tell. The two of us will have fun together, like old
times."

I didn't want to go. I wasn't the outdoor type. And
the place sounded like it might be creepy. But Barry
knew they'd never let him go alone—that was why
he was cajoling me. And I couldn't resist him. I
missed the closeness we used to have. And I didn't
have the heart to disagree with him now. "Sure," I
said. "It would be really great."

"Maybe that's not such a bad idea. . . ." Dad said.

Mom got up to clear the table, but just stood
there. "I *suppose* it could work," she said. "It would
be healthy for the twins to be out of the city, and I
can't imagine what kind of trouble they could get into
in a cornfield. I just . . . have a funny feeling about it.
Uncle Ambrose was such a character."

"What difference does that make now? He's dead,
isn't he?" Barry said.

Mom ignored him. "What was that story my mother told me? It was so long ago. . . . A lawsuit, with a
neighboring farmer. The farmer made some sort of
strange claim about Uncle Ambrose and his livestock. It didn't make a lot of sense, because Uncle
Ambrose wasn't a farmer, he had no interest in
livestock. But there was something unsavory about
the case. Now what was it?" She frowned.

"Who won?" Barry asked her.

"Uncle Ambrose won. He bragged about it for the rest of his life, my mother said. . . . Now it's coming back to me. The farmer claimed his cows wandered over there and came back shrunken and dry. But he could never prove it. Uncle Ambrose was supposedly eccentric, I guess, and a black sheep and everything. But why would he hurt somebody's cows?"

Barry flashed a glance at me. He was excited. Sushan, we both knew, was probably the dullest town in the world. But this Uncle Ambrose sounded more peculiar than anyone else in Mom's family. Some of his personality might have spilled over into his house. To Barry, it would be an adventure to explore the house, taking the keys and opening the various doors one by one. Certainly it would be better than staying home and being scrutinized by fussy adults.

"Mother used to tell me that Uncle Ambrose gloated about the case every time their mother dragged her to visit him, ridiculing that poor farmer. He had a vindictive streak. Maybe it had something to do with losing his fortune in the crash. That was what aged him. He looked sixty when he was forty."

Barry folded his hand tightly around the keys.

2

Getting to Sushan was complicated. From Chicago, we were to take a little commuter airline to a place called Champaign and from there, a long ride on a local bus to Sushan.

Travel always made me nervous, which Barry thought was stupid of me. And then there was Fred, who considered the whole experience an incomprehensible horror show. Fred was our dog—part cocker spaniel, part mutt. He would enjoy being in the country, and he could also act as a watchdog for us, Mom believed. Barry and I knew that Fred was more afraid of night noises than we were, but it would be fun to have him around. And he'd be good company for me if Barry went off into one of his moods.

Except that it was me who had to lug Fred, whimpering in his little carrier box, through the endless miles of O'Hare Airport. We finally reached the Wabash Airlines gate shortly before the plane took off. I was relieved for about one minute. Then I saw the plane. It was a tiny prop job, smaller than the average station wagon, with barely enough room inside for eight cramped seats. To the other passengers, plump, pink-faced and crew-cut, it all seemed routine. But I was horribly uncomfortable as we strapped ourselves in, and Fred, on my lap was very noisily beside himself. I tried to quiet him down, but once we started moving, it didn't matter anymore. The contraption bounced down the runway like a defective toy, its gasping engine making more noise than four jets ever did. We dipped alarmingly as the plane struggled into the sky, the floor and windowpanes buzzing like crazy. The lurching and rolling stopped when we reached our cruising altitude of about a hundred feet, though the noisy rattling did not—and Fred kept moaning.

Barry was sitting across the aisle from me, but he was so close that he leaned over easily to scream in my ear, "Can't you make that stupid animal shut up?"

"I'm doing the best I can!" I screamed back.

"Calm down," Barry said with contempt. "We're not going over any mountains."

An understatement. The landscape below us was so amazingly flat that it formed a natural checkerboard. The roads met at right angles and stretched rigidly across the countryside without curve or dip. It was as though no one had realized that there was any angle but ninety degrees, or any shape but a rectangle. The pattern was broken only by the isolated farmhouses and the curves of their trees. The frail, cigar-shaped shadow of the plane rippled over the textured squares of brown and green.

From the air, the landscape was too grandly surreal to be monotonous. But no grandeur was evident

9

from the windows of the bus, only endless rows of tall corn whizzing by, and the singsong dip and rise of telephone wires. The sheer numbing bleakness of it depressed me—so different from the rolling and populous East. The passengers on the bus were even plumper and pinker than their airborne counterparts. I nudged Barry and then grimaced at the placid faces around us, hoping to reestablish closeness by sharing our superiority to all these others. We were from the cultured, sophisticated, historical part of the country, after all. But Barry barely acknowledged my look. He was still irritated by my childish behavior on the plane.

Fred's cage was on my lap. He was more used to busses, and I bent down so he could lick my face, which helped a little to make up for Barry's unjust coldness. Reading on busses makes me carsick, so I looked out the window, tried to content myself with the cornfields and listened to my portable tape player. I wondered, each time we passed the farmhouse, if that was what Uncle Ambrose's house would be like.

"Soo-shan!" the bus driver finally called out. We struggled from the bus with Fred and our suitcases, and stepped out into the center of town. It was one block long. There were a couple of old brick buildings with flat facades and some white frame houses. Nothing was more than two stories high. The place looked dead, except for the dairy bar down at the end of the block to our right. There were six cars in its gravel parking lot and a group of men in big hats slouching beside them.

"Thank God we didn't get here during rush hour!" Barry said.

We were standing in front of one of the brick buildings. Deluxe Cafe was written over the doorway in unlit neon, and a cardboard sign in the dusty window advertised catfish sandwiches. The weeds that had broken through the cement sidewalk were as tall as my waist.

There wasn't even a rustle of wind in the towering old trees that lined the street. The only sound was the hum of the departing bus. It remained visible on the straight road, getting smaller and smaller, trembling in the waves of heat from the pavement. Suddenly I felt deserted, lonely. I looked at Barry and shrugged. He quickly turned away. "No sign of that lawyer guy," he said.

The lawyer had agreed over the phone to meet us and drive us to the house, explaining that it would be simpler than trying to find a cab. The toy-sized bus was the only moving object to the right. To the left, a railroad track cut across the road at the end of the block. On the other side was a row of peculiar white cylindrical structures, several stories taller than the brick buildings, and beyond them, cornfields. The road was empty in that direction.

"Maybe there's a pay phone in this place," Barry said, peering through the window of the Deluxe Cafe.

"It looks closed," I said. "I wonder if I should let Fred out. He must have to go something fierce."

"Don't. He'll just— Look, maybe that's the lawyer." A long, shiny, dark blue car pulled out from the other side of the dairy bar. It rolled over and stopped right in front of us. A middle-aged man in a business suit and sunglasses climbed out and closed the door, leaving the motor running. "Afternoon. You the Krasner boys?"

"Yeah, that's—" we started to say together. Barry shot me a look and I closed my mouth. "Yeah, that's us," Barry said.

The lawyer pulled off his glasses and looked curiously back and forth between us. His lips parted and he shook his head. "Twins, huh? Jeez, you *gotta* be! You two could be one kid holding a mirror. Never seen two separate people look so much alike."

"I'm Barry Krasner, and this is my brother Harry," Barry said, extending his hand in an impatient gesture.

Barry hated being a twin. I felt it every time someone mentioned our resemblance or called him by my name. To Barry, all my little flaws—and who doesn't have flaws?—were magnified and reflected back at him. When he looked at me, it was as though he were looking into a nasty, distorting mirror. And he was stuck with that mirror; it would always be with him. Even when we grew up and moved away from one another, even if we never saw each other, he would always know that I existed, somewhere, a living reminder of everything he hated about himself and couldn't change.

Sometimes I even thought Barry wanted me to die. What other escape from me was there?

"I bet even your own mother doesn't know one of you from the other," the lawyer went on, ignoring

Barry's extended hand, still impressed by our resemblance. "I bet she can't tell which is which."

"Mr. Crane!" Barry said, almost in a tone of reprimand, and grabbed his hand urgently and pumped it.

"That's me." The lawyer shook hands with me. "Well, might's well get goin'," he said, tearing his eyes away from us to glance at his watch. "Hope you two got the keys I sent."

"I have them," Barry said.

Barry took the front seat, and I got in back with Fred and the suitcases. The car was roomy and air-conditioned. Even so, we could feel the sudden burst of heat as we left the shady main street and bumped across the tracks.

"The town's kind of like an oasis in the middle of all these fields," Barry said. "Cool, because of the trees, I mean."

"Oasis! You mean like in a desert?" Mr. Crane shook his head. "You got it all wrong. This is the *prairie*." He spoke the word as though there was something amazing and beautiful about all this flatness, as though it were a mountain range or an ocean. "Desert? Why, the Illinois prairie is the most fertile land in the world. Nothing grows anywhere like it does here. Look at this corn. It's just turned August and already it's so tall you can't—"

I lurched against the front seat as Mr. Crane slammed on the brakes. We stopped about a foot from an old truck that had suddenly appeared out of nowhere and was rattling serenely across the highway in a cloud of dust. We could see, now, in the middle of the intersection, that a gravel road crossed the highway at right angles. A little street sign, partially hidden by an ear of corn, said 1800 N.

"This is a blind corner," I said, my heart pounding. "There should be a stop sign."

"Only blind at this time of year," Mr. Crane said. "Usually you can see anything coming along that road for miles. But not when the corn's high. It grows so fast it makes the road different. Gotta be careful. The corn always causes a lot of accidents this time of year."

"Killer corn, huh?" Barry said wryly.

"Yeah, you might say that," Mr. Crane said. "Sorry for the jolt." He wiped a hand across his forehead, and the car moved forward again.

Only a mile or so down the highway, we turned off onto another gravel road labeled 1500 N. We headed toward a line of trees—the first trees we'd seen since leaving the town. The road sloped downward and actually began to curve. Now there were dense banks of purple wildflowers along the road. We crossed a little concrete bridge, and a hundred yards later, a little metal bridge and after another hundred yards, a third bridge.

"So many streams, all so close together," Barry murmured, looking out the window to catch a glimpse of the water.

"It's all the same one, the Salt Fork River. Winds around a lot, that's all. Almost there."

We could see sections on the right of a falling-apart wooden fence almost completely buried under thick foliage. We turned onto a rutted dirt road. Leaves and branches scraped against the car as we passed through an opening in a high, brambly hedge. "Can't stop trimming this stuff for a week even," Mr. Crane murmured. Past the hedge, the two tracks of the road faded out of existence into a weedy, overgrown meadow before they even reached the house. "Could be a nice place, right on the river and all, if somebody'd put some money into it," said Mr. Crane, and he reached for the ignition.

We stepped out of the car as the motor died. It wasn't silent here. The meadow buzzed with insect sounds. Though they came from all sides, the individual whining voices rose and fell together in the same unvarying rhythm, as though all the thousands of them were following the beat of one conductor.

The wooden house had been white once; the roofs, green. There was a long front porch and a round bay at one end of it that rose to become a sort of tower with a conical roof. Intricate but neglected wooden gingerbread carvings curled along the porch roof and around the variously shaped windows and the steep, sloping eaves. The house at first gave the impression of being quite large. Then you realized that it was small, just very complicated.

There was about forty feet of meadow between the house and the row of trees behind it—the same trees we had been traveling toward since we left the main road. It was late afternoon now, and the tree shadows had almost reached the house. If you listened closely, you could hear, underneath the grating insects, the cool splashing of water over stones.

Barry was staring around with his chin lifted and

his mouth half-open, his hands clenched by his sides. If Mr. Crane hadn't been there, Barry would have been hooting and jumping up and down like a little kid. He was in love with the place already—I could sense it as clearly as I could hear the insects.

"Hey, isn't this wonderful? I just love it!" I said, wanting to be included in his excitement. I didn't say anything about how run-down the place was or how isolated—we hadn't passed another house since leaving town. It was already dark under those trees. Would the phone be working? What about the electricity?

"Here we are, Fred," I said as brightly as I could. I pulled his cage out of the car and opened it up. He tore out of it, hopped wildly around me, barking, then suddenly stopped, sniffed the air, and took off, his long ears flying behind him. In seconds, he was hidden by the tall meadow grasses.

"Cute dog." Mr. Crane cleared his throat. "Hope nothing happens to him."

"What?" Barry turned back to him, taking his eyes from the house for the first time since we'd stepped out of the car. "What did you say?"

"Time for me to get going," said Mr. Crane. He looked at his watch. "You boys okay now? Got the keys and all?"

"We're fine," Barry said enthusiastically, no longer able to keep from grinning. "We're going to have a *great* time!"

"Well, I made sure the food was delivered, like your folks asked," he said, pulling open the car door. "Nice to meet you."

"Thanks, thanks a lot," we both told him. "We'll be fine," Barry insisted. He was so eager for Mr. Crane to leave that he looked like he had to pee. He turned back to the house, reaching into his pocket for the keys.

I leaned into the front window of the car as Mr. Crane started the motor. "Can we call you, if...we need to?" I asked him, softly so Barry wouldn't hear.

"Sure." He turned the car around and headed back to the road. As the motor faded, I wondered how long it would be before we heard that sound again.

I turned back to the house. Barry was at the front door. He was going to go in without even waiting for me. "Hey, wait a minute!" I called as I ran toward him, hoping he'd hear me over the insects. I almost tripped on the porch steps, which were partially hidden by weeds.

"Harry, did you ever *see* any place as great as this? The river, and the meadow, and everything! And this crazy old house. And it's all ours for the next two weeks! It's like...I don't know *what* it's like!"

"Like a dream," I said cornily, watching Barry try the keys in the front door. It occurred to me that Uncle Ambrose must have been dead for a long time before anyone found him. And what condition had he been in then?

"This is the one," Barry said as the third key slid smoothly into the lock. He gave it a couple of twists. The lock clicked. He pushed open the door.

3

It was dark inside the narrow front hall after the glare outside, but we could see the stairway directly in front of us and openings to other rooms on the left and right. I turned back and found the light switch by the door. It was an old-fashioned one with two buttons, but the glass fixture in the middle of the ceiling still worked.

"Oh, wow," came Barry's awestruck murmur from the room on the right. "Will you just look at this."

It was even darker in this room because of the front porch that shaded the window. But there was another working light fixture, more elaborate, with curving brass rods and cut-glass shades. The room was jammed with old furniture—Victorian couches and fat, sagging chairs and little tables and an ornate marble fireplace. But it was not Uncle Ambrose's furniture collection that Barry was exclaiming about.

For a second I thought they were just a lot of white figurines. Then I saw that they were skeletons,

18

dozens of them, carefully mounted, displayed on every surface.

I made a kind of grunting laugh. "I don't believe this," I said. The one closest to me, beside a stained-glass lamp on a little table, might have been a squirrel. It had a long tail and sharp little teeth, and squatted on its hind legs, supported by metal braces like an exhibit in a museum. There were several cases with glass doors, and other skeletons were splayed on boards and hung on the walls.

"No wonder people thought he was eccentric," I said, remaining in the doorway.

"Hey! This thing has *six legs*!" Barry shouted, from a case at the dark back end of the room.

"Don't do that, Barry." I fought the impulse to dash from the house. "No animal has six legs."

"Come and see for yourself."

I went reluctantly, hoping it was just one of his mean tricks. But he was right. The thing looked like a cat skeleton, except for the extra pelvis and pair of legs in the middle. I felt sick.

"And look at this. A snake with a bird's head. See the beak? Exotic animals they have here in Illinois." Barry chuckled and shook his head. "The old guy sure had a weird sense of humor—putting parts of different skeletons together to make them look like monsters."

"You think that's what these are?" I said, relieved.

"What else?" He was delighted. "Too bad there's no human bones. But who knows what we'll find in the rest of the house?"

I wished he hadn't said that, but I laughed again—if I showed any sign of being a sissy, Barry would turn hateful. "If there *are* human ones, wouldn't they be hidden?" I said as we trooped back across the hall. "I mean, so people wouldn't wonder where they came from?"

"There's no law against having human skeletons in your house," Barry pointed out.

But the dining-room table was covered only with piles of dusty books and magazines—including, as Dad had predicted, lots of *National Geographics*. And the kitchen was almost cozy, with its wooden table and old gas stove and freestanding porcelain sink, all the pipes exposed underneath. A wall phone was mounted over the table. When Barry wasn't looking, I checked to make sure it was working. It was.

Behind the kitchen was a little workroom that in a normal house would have been a gardening or tool shed—its screen door led to the meadow behind the house. But clearly it had been Uncle Ambrose's mounting room. The cubbyholes on the old worktable were neatly filled with little pins and metal rods and various delicate tools, and there were bottles of cleaning solutions and a stack of mounting boards. A bat skeleton, which Uncle Ambrose had apparently been working on when he died, was taking shape on the worktable. The fierce little head and the leathery wings and the rib cage were attached to the board, but the rest of the skeleton lay in piles beside it, waiting to be affixed.

"Well, that proves it," Barry said. "He was a

do-it-yourselfer. Wonder how he came up with the raw materials. They're all in perfect condition."

We went upstairs. There was a large front bedroom with a lumpy-looking double bed. "Dibs on not sleeping in Uncle Ambrose's room," I called quickly—it was an important enough issue to risk incurring Barry's contempt.

But he didn't hold it against me. "It would be kind of weird, sleeping in a room where somebody died," he agreed. But then he had to add, "People probably died in *all* the bedrooms in old houses—probably died in our bedrooms at home."

There were a couple of smaller bedrooms, a bathroom as archaic as the kitchen and a locked door. Barry tried the keys and a moment later pulled it open, to reveal a narrow and steep flight of steps. He grinned. "Maybe there *will* be a human one up here," he said.

I knew he was trying to scare me, and that was exactly why I couldn't back down. I followed close behind him. There were a couple of dusty windows, and a bare bulb, and nothing peculiar stored under the eaves, I was glad to see—more piles of magazines, boxes of books and broken chairs. The only object at all intriguing to Barry was a metal box about a foot square sitting by itself in the middle of the attic floor.

Again, he tried the keys. Again, it didn't take him long to get it open. There were a few books inside, a small bundle of letters, and a key. The key was attached by a wire to a small piece of cardboard with the word *play* neatly printed on it.

"Funny," I said. "What do you think it could mean?"

"A playhouse maybe? Out in back somewhere?"

"Want to look for it?" I had had enough of this house for the time being. "We should go outside anyway and find Fred before it gets dark."

"Okay. And we can check out the river too, and see if there's a swimming hole." Barry kept the little key, locked up the box and locked the attic door too.

The meadow behind the house was in shade now, the sun had dropped behind the trees and the sky was deepening in color. Fred came yapping to greet us and trotted along beside us as we followed the sounds of water. The steep riverbank was thick with scratchy underbrush. Barry slid and stumbled down, and I picked my way carefully behind.

I stood beside him on a gravel bank, and we stared down at the hurrying water. When the trees moved in the wind, patches of sunlight trembled and dazzled on the river's shady surface. It was so shallow that we could see the pebbly bottom all the way to the opposite bank, twenty feet away. "Hardly even deep enough for wading," I said.

"Shhh!" Barry pointed upstream to the left. About forty feet from us, the river curved and a small cliff rose out of the water, maybe fifteen feet high. It was a double cliff, reversed upon itself in the black pool beneath, where the water was so still it was like a dark mirror. Then the pale figure, which I had thought was part of the rock formation, lunged forward, rose and fell and met itself on the surface. The reflection dissolved.

A moment later a head appeared among the ripples. Fred barked, and the head became a face.

My first impulse was to turn away and pretend we hadn't been spying. But Barry lifted his hand in a casual greeting. There was a pause. Then the person in the water waved back slowly and immediately dived again.

Hot and sweaty as I was, the dark pool did not seem inviting to me. "I don't feel like swimming, but you go right ahead," I urged Barry. "I'll just—"

"Can't you see she isn't wearing anything?" Barry said impatiently. "I had to wave, so she wouldn't think we're a couple of Peeping Toms. But I bet we scared her anyway."

"She doesn't seem to care," I said, trying to mollify him. "She's just calmly swimming around."

"What do you expect her to do? Get *out*, with the two of us standing here?" He turned away abruptly. "Come on, jerk." He started up the slope. "Let's see if there's a playhouse to go with this key."

I couldn't see what I had done wrong this time—maybe it was just the fact of being my twin that was annoying Barry again.

We stepped out from under the trees onto the meadow. The sky was amazing. Fat, heavy clouds, orange-shaded, were piled up in layers that went on and on forever, like mountains shrinking into the distance. The horizon was a lot farther away here than in the East.

"There," Barry said, pointing at a neat circle of

pines between the house and the river. "Maybe it's in there."

We walked through waist-high grass toward the pines. I felt uneasy under this tremendous sky. It was a luminous ocean suspended above us, full of movement and life and danger. The raucous insects were louder than ever. Their incessant pulsating song rose into a kind of frenzy, silvery and demented.

"They're singing at the sunset," I whispered, not wanting to disturb them. "Chanting for the day to end."

Barry laughed. "Sure. And maybe if something stopped them, then the sun would stop too."

Ahead of us, Fred dashed through the one narrow gap in the circle of trees. The grass was shorter here, as though it had been mowed recently. We paused just outside the pines, where there was a sundial. It was useless now, in the shade. "Funny place for a sundial," I said. "Too close to the trees."

Barry stepped inside the circle. The insects rose suddenly in volume, screaming harshly from the pine trees.

And there *was* a playhouse. It was a nondescript rectangular building with a sloping roof, about twelve feet long by six feet wide. What was odd was that it was in much better condition than the real house, clean and freshly painted, with a new-looking shiny aluminum roof. The door that faced us from one of the ends of the building was also made of metal and seemed out of place, as though it belonged on a bomb shelter rather than a playhouse. While Fred sniffed and scratched at the door, I followed Barry around the building. We saw that there were no windows and no other door. We looked it over slowly and thoroughly. Against the back wall was a funny-looking thing with pipes and valves that might have been a pump. Beside it stood a large wooden crate, unlocked, containing dozens of big batteries. They didn't tell us much. We returned to the front of the building.

Barry took the little key from the attic out of his pocket. He pushed Fred away from the door and slid the key into the lock. He turned it, the lock clicked and he pushed at the door. It didn't open.

"That's funny," Barry said. "It fits okay." He shook the door, he pushed it, he pulled it. It wouldn't budge.

"Maybe it was labeled wrong," I said.

"Yeah, maybe." He took the key ring out of his pocket and began trying the other keys.

Fred was still sniffing and scratching at the door. I pulled him aside so that Barry wouldn't get mad at him for being in the way, and kneeled down to cuddle with him. "Seems like Fred wants to get inside as much as you do," I said.

Barry looked at me, frowning. He wasn't having any luck with the keys. "Didn't Mr. Crane say something about Fred?" he asked me.

"Did he?"

"Yes. Something like a warning. Don't you remember?"

"He did say Fred was cute, I think," I told him, doing my best to remember. "And then he said it was time for him to go."

"Yes, but *before* he said it was time to go, he said something else about Fred, like he hoped he wouldn't get hurt or anything. Come on, Harry, help me remember."

"He said Fred was cute," I said, thinking hard. "And then he said he had to go, and asked us about the keys. But he never—"

"Oh, forget it!" Barry snapped, turning back to the door.

"Don't get mad," I unwisely protested. "I'm just telling you what I remember he—"

"'Don't get mad'!" he mimicked me, furiously jamming keys at the lock. "What do you expect me to do? The few times it seems like it *might* be an advantage having you around, like you *might* be able to help me remember what somebody said, that's when you— Oh, forget it!" He straightened up and threw down the keys. "None of them fits." He shook the playhouse door by its metal handle, then he kicked it. It didn't even quiver. "If there is a key, it's somewhere else."

"Then we'll find it," I said, trying to keep the hurt out of my voice. I picked up the keys and held them out to him. "We'll have plenty of time to look for it. We don't have anything else to do."

Barry sighed and took back the keys, "I guess so. . . ."

Then Fred was barking—his worried bark, the bark that meant strangers.

"You hear anybody?" Barry whispered.

"No, but Fred must have."

"A squirrel or something," Barry said, and he stepped out of the circle.

Someone cried out. I had the absurd notion of the monster cat skeleton from the living room attacking. I was nervous, but I couldn't give Barry another chance to ridicule me. I forced myself to follow him.

4

It was almost dark now. But I could see a girl standing by the sundial, a pink towel wrapped around her head and a hand over her mouth.

She removed the hand and pressed it to her throat. She started to speak. Then she saw me, and she jumped.

"What's the matter?" Barry said.

"Oh . . . twins!" She laughed. She wore faded jeans and a T-shirt, and her face, beneath the towel, was rather flat and snub-nosed. But she was still pretty. "Don't think I'm silly," she said. "I didn't hear voices, so I didn't think nobody was close by. And then all of a sudden *you* come out of nowhere"—she looked at Barry—"and then, it was like the same person showed up all over again. I couldn't tell you two look exactly alike, down by the river."

The insects were slowing down, like a drowsing organism, the voices dropping out one by one. Now, hundreds of tiny flickering lights bobbed and darted through the dark meadow. "Gee, there must be more fireflies right here in this yard than I've ever seen before in my whole life," Barry said, moving the conversation away from our resemblance, as usual.

"Where you guys from?" the girl said. "You talk funny."

"Boston," Barry said.

"Never knew anybody from there," the girl said. "You relations of old man Kittery, or what?"

"Yes, we inherited his house," Barry explained. "My brother and I came to sort of watch over the house for a couple weeks until our parents can get here and go through the stuff to see if there's anything worth keeping."

"Like all them dead animal bones?" she said with a derisive little laugh.

"You know?" Barry asked her.

"Sure." She shrugged. "Everybody's been peeking in the windows since the old man died." She peered around Barry, past the sundial into the circle of trees. It was too dark now to see anything but the glint of the playhouse's metal roof. "You got a set of keys, I see." Her voice quickened. "You get into the playhouse? See what's inside?"

Barry glanced at me. "Why?" he asked her. "What's supposed to be inside it?"

"Don't know," she said guardedly. "That's why I'm asking you."

Barry thought for a moment, trying to decide what to tell her. So far, I hadn't said a word. "No," Barry said. "None of these keys fits. But there must a key somewhere inside the big house—and I'm going to find it."

"Well, when you do, will you tell me what's inside the playhouse?" she said, her voice eager again. "I'd be real curious to know."

"What makes you think there'd be anything but a lot of old tools and stuff?"

"Oh . . . Just because," she said.

"Because what?" Barry demanded.

"Like what I said, I'm just curious. What's wrong with that?" she said, evading his question. She adjusted the towel on her head.

"Well, why should I tell you what's in there if you won't tell *me* why you're curious about it?" Barry said, beginning to sound annoyed.

"Hey, come on, Barry, it's getting kind of late," I said. I didn't want him to start arguing with her.

"So what? We're on our own. Nobody's telling us what to do, or when. I'll stay out here all night if I feel like it. *You* can go call up Mom and ask her what time to go to bed if you want."

I blushed. Barry really knew how to make me feel stupid in front of other people. It was what he did whenever I tried to argue with him.

"Are you guys ever lucky," the girl said. "Your folks let you come all the way from Boston, and stay in a crazy old house like that all by yourselves. Do anything you want, no chores, no rules." She made a whistling sound of genuine envy.

"Want to come in and see the house?" Barry said, his irritation suddenly gone. "If you tell us what you know about this place, we'll show you around. I'll take you inside the playhouse if I get in."

"The playhouse—I don't know about going *in*. But the house, sure."

"And you'll tell us what you know?" Barry pressed her.

"Well, yeah, but..." She seemed hesitant again.

"But why *not*?"

"Well, but if you're the old man's family, you might not like the kinda things I..." Her voice dwindled away.

"Look," Barry told her. "He was a relative that we never met and hardly even *heard* of, practically, until he died and left our mother this house. It's not like we have any kind of loyalty to him. We heard he was weird and unpopular around here. We're not going to be insulted or anything. We just want to find out about him." He grinned his most charming grin at her—he hadn't looked at me that way for years. "Doesn't that make sense?"

"Well... yeah, I guess, when you put it that way." She thought for a moment, pursing her lips. "What difference does it make now, anyway? He's dead, ain't he? Come on, let's go."

But I wasn't sure it was a good idea to invite her in. We'd hardly been inside the house for half an hour ourselves and hadn't explored it thoroughly. What if something happened to her? And who was she, anyway? Would it be wise to show her what was in the house? Would our parents, or Mr. Crane, have approved? And I wasn't sure I liked her very much. She seemed ignorant and pushy. If she started hanging around all the time, our two weeks could be ruined. "You don't have to go home for supper or anything?" I said.

They turned back, already moving toward the house. "Oh, Harry!" Barry said, sounding hostile and embarrassed at the same time.

"We already ate, ages ago," the girl said. It was too dark to see her expression, but I caught the tinge of disparagement in her voice. Already she didn't like me. "My folks know I'm just out around the farm somewhere, didn't even take my bike or nothing. I got a good hour before they'll start wanting me back."

"Your parents are farmers?" Barry said as they started walking again.

"Uh huh. We own all the fields around here, across the river and on the other side of the road too. It's been in the family since my great-grandfather. The Kittery place is kind of like a little island in the middle—the river makes a loop right around it."

"You'd think your family would have tried to buy it," Barry said. They had already forgotten about me.

"Yeah, except this little meadow here never was much good for corn. Down low by the river and all, and full of boulders. The earth's too thin here, with a granite shelf right underneath it. 'Course, that's not to say they didn't try to buy it, one time or another. . . . Just 'cause it was kind of a nuisance, having it here."

"Wait a minute." Barry stopped and turned to face her just outside the back door. "That must mean it was one of *your* relatives who sued Uncle Ambrose."

"I thought you said you weren't gonna get insulted or anything."

"Who said I was insulted? I'm just interested in the story, that's all."

Barry led the way inside, turning on lights. I left them to examine the mounting room and went ahead into the kitchen. I dug through the boxes of food that had been delivered and fed Fred. Then I tried to figure out what to do about our supper. I was ravenous.

"Hey, Barry, would you like some tomato soup and a toasted cheese sandwich?" I asked him when they came through the kitchen.

"Uh, sure," Barry said as if he hadn't really heard me.

The girl pulled the towel off her head. Her hair was short and curly and blonde, and she had freckles. She looked about our age.

"So old-fashioned in here," she said, draping the towel over a chair.

"Wait'll you see the living room," Barry said. "Come on."

I listened to their muffled voices and the floors creaking under their footsteps as I warmed up soup and peeled slices of cheese out of plastic. Fred, after gobbling his food, lay down on the floor and watched me, flapping his little tail on the rug. "Good boy, Fred. We're friends, aren't we," I told him, and squatted down frequently to pet him.

They came back to the kitchen about twenty minutes later. Old-fashioned as it was, it was the only remotely inviting room in the house, without skeletons or piles of books everywhere. The stained wooden table was comfortable for sitting around, and there was a round rag rug on the floor.

"*That's* the way *you* heard it? Sheesh!" the girl was saying as they came in.

"It's just what our mother thought she remembered *her* mother said when Mom was a little girl. None of us was ever involved in it or cared about it."

The girl clucked her tongue. "Boy, my grandpa sure did," she said.

"What was his version?" Barry asked her.

She pursed her little round mouth humorously and rolled her eyes to the side.

"Come on, sit down and tell us," Barry said. "You promised."

"Okay." Her hesitation vanished instantly. She plopped down on a chair and leaned forward on her elbows. "I grew up with it. My grandpa talked about it all the time. And every time you started to forget about it, there was *this* place, right in the middle of everything, to remind you."

"Yeah? Go on," Barry said, sitting down across from her.

"Well, now we do mostly just corn and soybeans, but in the old days, Grandpa kept a lot of livestock too, cows and pigs, mostly. He loved them animals, not like a lot of farmers, who just think of them like another crop. Grandpa even named them. He was funny that way. But don't get me wrong, he wasn't no nut case like old man Kittery— Oh, sorry about that."

"I told you, we never even knew him."

"Naming his animals doesn't seem so funny to

me," I said, with a glance at Fred. "You don't mind if we eat?" I asked her, setting down bowls and plates.

"Uh uh. Anyway, he had this sow, name of Estelle. She'd won all these prizes, he was so proud of that pig. My dad used to have to wash her and brush her up. Well, then one morning she was gone. She'd got out of her pen and wandered away. They were sure they'd find her—you don't just lose a 400-pound sow, they're big. And they found tracks in the underbrush, like she'd gone down to the river and up the other side, over here. But when they came over to look, old man Kittery told them he never seen her; she hadn't been here. He let them look around, and she weren't there."

"Did they look inside the playhouse?" Barry asked.

"Wasn't no playhouse then, just those trees and a big flat rock there."

"When did he build the playhouse, I wonder?"

"I'm coming to that. Anyway, they never found Estelle, just had to give up. But Grandpa was mad. A pig like that's worth a lot of money."

"But couldn't somebody else have stolen the pig?" Barry said.

"They saw the tracks coming right over here. And then after that, there was Giselle, a cow, and her calf, Artichoke. Same thing happened to them, tracks coming over here and everything. Never found them again. After that, Grandpa built a double barbed-wire fence all around this property."

"Maybe he *did* steal the animals, and butchered them in there," Barry said, with a nod at the mounting room.

"You can't butcher big animals in a tiny place like that. And Grandpa knew everybody in town and for miles around. If Kittery had sold those animals, even cut up as meat, Grandpa would have known. Kittery didn't even have a truck to carry them or a car. No, there was no explanation except they disappeared over here. Even after the double fence, Cavity got out and never came back."

"Cavity?" I said. "What kind of a name is that?"

"Cavity was a beautiful horse. When he disappeared, it was all Grandma could do to keep Grandpa from coming over here and shooting Kittery dead. And that was when he got the idea to set a trap and catch Kittery in the act—whatever the act was. So on purpose he didn't fix the hole in the fence where Cavity got through. And then he got all the hands to stay up with him and watch. And they waited. And on the third night, along comes Emptiness and goes right through the fence and down—"

"Emptiness!" I interrupted. "He really named an animal Emptiness?"

"His best milk cow. He thought it was kind of a joke to name her that. And she was as lazy and sluggish as they come. But *something* was attracting her over to this meadow here—maybe one of them whistles people can't hear. Anyway, she made enough noise trampling down to the river and across it that they didn't have any trouble sneaking quietly along behind. And they waited on this side and watched Emptiness go straight for that circle of pine trees. They could see, because there was light coming from them. And then, after five minutes, Grandpa gave the signal, and they all ran back there together, with lights. Grandpa even had a camera."

"Yeah? Go on," Barry urged her. He'd hardly touched his supper, and I didn't think there was anything wrong with it—I was already on my second helping. But I knew it would be a mistake to ask him if it was all right.

"Old man Kittery was standing there, and Emptiness."

"Was he doing anything wrong?"

"No." She leaned forward and said slowly and distinctly, *"Only Emptiness looked twenty years older.* She was all skinny and shrunk, with her udders withered and bones sticking out. And Kittery was furious, he started screaming for them to get off his land. And Grandpa was screaming at him to give him back his cow. And then—this is how they tell it— Kittery laughed, and pushed Emptiness away and said"—her voice changed—"'You call this old thing a cow? She's nothing but skin and bones. What would *I* want with her?'"

She recited the quotation like a familiar poem. Then she sat back and folded her arms and looked at Barry.

Even Barry couldn't think of anything to say. He shook his head. "Twenty years older?"

"But they all knew it was Emptiness, because of her markings. That's when Grandpa took him to court."

"It doesn't make any sense," Barry said.

She shrugged. "Who knows? I guess that's why the judge couldn't do anything. 'Course he wasn't on

37

Kittery's side—he warned him he'd be in trouble if there was any more complaints. And everybody else was ready to lynch him. And *that's* when he built the playhouse. And after that, the animals stopped disappearing."

"I don't believe it," Barry said. He took a big bite of his sandwich and gulped it down, not even tasting it. "They probably just stopped letting them run away. It was probably your grandpa's fault from the beginning. Why would building the playhouse change anything?"

"I knew you'd get mad," she said, flushing. "I probably shouldn't have told you." She stood up. "My folks would probably kill me if—"

"Wait a minute, don't go," Barry said slowly, putting his half-eaten sandwich down. "I just remembered something. Be right back." He hurried into the mounting room.

"Well, I can't stay *much* longer," the girl said, but she sat down again.

"I wonder if he had his skeleton collection then," I said. "I wonder if there is any connection between that and your grandpa's animals. It must have made people suspicious of Uncle Ambrose."

She looked in Barry's direction, then said desultorily, "He wasn't friendly. Nobody from around here ever went inside this house. Anyway, it wouldn't have made any difference, little skeletons of squirrels and mice and things, nothing that could have been our animals. This meadow here always had little skeletons anyway, the story is. The Illinois Indians had a funny name for it, that meant skeleton stone, I think."

"What's that?" Barry said, coming back into the kitchen. He leaned against the sink, something cupped in his hand.

"*Oobish* or something," she said, looking up at the beamed ceiling. "Skeleton stone, it meant. That's what the Indians used to call this meadow. We learned it in school."

"And your grandpa knew that and didn't wonder about it?"

"What's a few little rabbit bones have to do with losing a prize pig, a horse, a cow and its calf?" she said hotly, spinning around to Barry.

I hated arguments. "What's that in your hand?" I asked him, trying to calm things down.

"The key to the playhouse," he said. "Let's go."

□

5

"How do you know it's the right key?" the girl demanded. She wasn't flushed anymore; she was distinctly pale.

"I noticed it in that little room before. It has a tag that says House on it, see? So I just thought it was another house key. Then we found *this* one"—he took it out of his pocket—"that says Play on it. It fit the playhouse lock, but it didn't open the door. And I just realized—maybe you need both keys, Play and House, to get it to open. Come on, let's go take a look."

Barry has always been adventurous. He loves taking risks. That's one of the scary things about him—he can get out of control.

"Now?" I said. "Right now, you want to go there? Shouldn't we wait?"

"What for?" He tossed the keys in his palm and pushed himself away from the sink.

"Ain't it kinda late?" the girl said. "I mean, too dark to see much and all?"

"I've got a flashlight in my pack. It's upstairs."

"You know what time it is?" the girl asked me while Barry was out of the room.

I put down the fork I had been playing with and got out my calculator, which has a clock mode. "Nine fifteen," I said.

"You always so nervous and fidgety?" she asked me.

"I'm not nervous," I said, putting the calculator away and crumpling up my napkin in my lap. I wished I could make her like me better, but I couldn't think of anything to say. It was a relief when Barry returned with the red plastic flashlight.

Fred got up to follow us as we headed for the door. Barry stopped. "Maybe Fred better stay," he said.

"Why?" I said. I always felt more secure when Fred was around.

"You want him to come along, Harry?" Barry said, giving me a funny look. "Okay, sure, let him come."

It was dark outside the back door, and the night was full of the sounds of trees and water. There were only a few isolated fireflies now, and the other insects sang a subdued scratchy song that came in waves from the deeper blackness under the trees.

The girl held the flashlight on the door and I held Fred while Barry inserted the two keys, one after the other, moving the lock each time. He tried the door. It moved.

"But why does it need two keys?" I said.

"To make it harder to get in. Here, give me that." Barry took the flashlight, pushed open the door and directed the light inside.

Something that looked like a textured gray wall

filled the doorway opening. The beam of light penetrated the stuff unevenly, making a blotchy oval patch. Tentatively, Barry touched it. He pulled back his hand so quickly that I made a gasping noise. Thin strands clung to his fingers.

"Ugh! *Spiderwebs*," the girl said.

They were so thick they did make a kind of wall. "Never seen anything like this," Barry breathed. "Not in any basement or attic. Must mean no one's been inside for years and years."

"More like three weeks," the girl said. "The old man used to go in and out of here all the time, right up until he died. Used to see him myself."

Barry shook his head, and ran the flashlight over the grass. In a moment he found a long stick. He stuck it inside and swung it back and forth until he made a large opening in the cobwebs. Then, holding the stick and flashlight in front of him, he stepped inside.

The girl looked at me, then set her lips and followed him. I knew I had to go in too—there was no possible excuse. But just as I stepped over the threshold, I heard a noise and turned around. A small rabbit had stopped under the sundial. Fred barked and moved toward the rabbit.

"Well, I never!" the girl said, her voice muffled.

I turned back inside. My feet crunched down on some material that was brittle on the surface, sticky underneath.

Then Barry found the light, a single bulb with a pull chain in the center of the ceiling. In the breeze from the door, the cobwebs wafted against us like layers of gauze curtains. The floor was hidden by a solid layer of dead insects.

"Yuck!" the girl said, looking down at the floor, her arms wrapped around her. She pushed some of the insect bodies aside with the toe of her sneaker. "Glad I'm not barefoot, that's all I can say."

Barry was slashing at the cobwebs like a jungle explorer with a machete. "This always happen around here when you leave a place locked up for three weeks?" he asked her.

"Nope."

"It didn't happen inside the house, and that was empty just as long," I said.

"And this place is a lot tighter than that house," Barry said. "Why'd they fill this place up so *fast*?"

"Smells like about ten storm cellars all rolled into one," the girl said, wrinkling her nose.

It was true. The place had a moldy, ancient basement smell.

"Except it's so much newer than the house," Barry said. "Look."

There was a narrow metal cot and a chest of drawers along one of the long walls, and a table and chair and kitchen-type cabinet along the other. Against the back wall was a large sink, and in the corner to the right of it, a toilet, right out in the open. The furniture was all made out of metal, simple and functional and more modern than the things in the house. Barry took a couple of steps toward the end of the room, his feet crackling on the little corpses, and tapped the wall above the sink. "Metal," he said. "The whole place is made out of metal. Looks like he

43

fixed it up so he could come and live out here. But why all the metal?"

"Makes me think of a bomb shelter," I said.

"Except it's aboveground," Barry pointed out. "And who would think of a bomb shelter way back then?"

"I don't know." I shrugged. "But why would he want to come out here and stay?"

"*I* don't know," Barry said, and sighed. "But I swear I'll figure out what this place was for."

"Well, good luck to you," the girl said, with a short laugh. "I told you what I know about it—not that any of this stuff explains what happened to them animals." She looked around the room again and lifted her hands. "Well, I better be—"

"Hey, look at this." Barry pointed up to the ceiling with his stick. A square with hinges on one side was cut into the metal. He pulled the chair over, climbed up, and lifted his hands.

"Careful," I couldn't keep from saying.

The ceiling was so low that Barry had to bend over to stand on the chair. The trapdoor opened easily and fell back on the other side with a clang. "Hand me the flashlight," he said. Then he stood up and stuck his arms and head through. From underneath, we could see nothing up there but more cobwebs. A moment later Barry ducked down again and jumped from the chair, holding something. "Look at this," he said.

It was a green metal box, about the size of a package of tea bags, with black letters stenciled on it. U.S. Army. Survival Biscuits, it said. "Piles and piles of these up there under the rafters," Barry said. "And books, and more of those big batteries, one of them hooked up to the light. He really wanted to make sure he could hole up in here."

"But that still don't tell me what happened to the animals," the girl said. "And now I really gotta—"

There was a dull thud, and we all spun around. The door had slammed shut, perhaps in a gust of wind. I ran to push it open, but it wouldn't move. We were locked in.

At least I wasn't the only one who panicked. The girl and I were both beating on the door—until Barry pushed us away, holding up the keys. "We have to be careful," he said as he turned them in the lock and then opened the door. "It locks automatically—and you need the keys to get out and get in."

I was the first one out. The rabbit was hopping away from the sundial. Fred took off after it.

"Huh?" I said.

"Now what's the matter?" said Barry.

"The rabbit. It just ran away *now*, and Fred just ran after it."

"So? Dogs chase rabbits all the time."

"But they were in the same place when we went inside the playhouse."

"There's hundreds of rabbits around here," the girl said. "He chased one before, and then another one came along and he chased it too."

"But . . ."

"What else could have happened, Harry?" Barry said.

"Well, I really gotta get going," the girl said. She

backed away, lifting her hand to wave at Barry, " 'Bye now."

"You never told me your name," Barry said.

"Lucy," she said. "Lucy Coolidge. And you're Barry and Harry . . ."

"Barry Krasner."

"Nice to meet you. 'Bye. See you later." She hurried off toward the river.

Barry was fresh and rested the next morning. He whistled as he showered and very carefully shaved. After breakfast he announced that we would clean the bugs and spiderwebs out of the playhouse. I would have been happy if we never set foot in that place again. But, as usual, I went along with what he wanted to do.

We brought two brooms and a dustpan and some garbage bags out to the playhouse. Barry began on the cobwebs, and I started sweeping up the bugs. There was a lot of silvery dust on the floor as well as dead insects.

After about ten minutes I had a substantial pile. "Where're the bags?" I asked Barry.

"Huh?" Barry looked around. "Oh, I guess I put them down when I unlocked the door. They must still be outside." He was standing on the metal chair, brushing cobwebs out of the back corner of the ceiling—the walls were still thickly draped with them. I had cleared about one square yard of floor; the rest was black with insect bodies.

"Where're the keys?" I said.

"Right there on the table."

I took the keys and let myself out. Shading my eyes, I looked around for Fred. Then I bent over to get the bags, and the door slammed shut behind me. "Darn thing!" I said, and unlocked it again.

I stepped back inside. "We've got to do something about this door, it's a real—"

My voice died. Barry wasn't standing on the chair. He lay on the cot in his underwear, asleep, his mouth half-open, his eyes closed. His clothes were piled on the floor beside the dresser. There were no cobwebs anywhere, and the stone floor was clear of bugs, except for a mountain of them near where I stood at the door.

Barry had heard me start my sentence. His eyes fluttered open and came to rest on me.

There was pale stubble on the lower half of his face.

6

An instant later Barry was out of bed and had me pinned against the wall. "Where the hell were you? How could you leave me locked up in here all night?" He shook me. "What's the matter with you? How could you leave me locked in here? You jerk! Say something!" He shook me again.

"Ouch! Stop it, stop it! I didn't!" I pushed him off and backed away from him.

"How could you do that to me? You knew I couldn't get out! I could *kill* you!" He was panting, his face distorted.

"But I didn't, Barry," I said, frightened. "I just went and got the bags, like I said." I thrust the bags at him. "I went out and the door slammed, that's all. I was only gone for a second."

He came at me again. "You lying, sissy-brained—"

"You weren't in here overnight!" I screamed. "It's the same day!"

"You're stupid, but you're not crazy!" He reached for me.

I lifted my hands to fend him off, cowering back

toward the table. "Please, Barry, it *is* the same day! Why would I lock you in here overnight?"

"Who knows?" He pushed my shoulder.

I fell back against the table. My hand knocked something noisily to the floor—a tin of the survival biscuits, half-empty. Paper wrappings lay crushed on the table. "You ate these things?" I said.

"What did you expect me to do? Go hungry, you jerk?" Barry took a deep breath. He stepped away from me and sat down on the bed. "It's a good thing the toilet works." He grunted. "I can't *believe* you did this."

"But Barry, I didn't do *anything*." I was close to tears now. "I just stepped out and got the bags. I wasn't even gone for a minute. Why won't you believe me?"

"Believe you?" He gestured around the room. "It took me hours to clean this place up." He looked down at his half-naked body, and the pile of clothes. "I went to sleep." He reached up to touch the fuzz on his face. "I need to shave. And you're trying to tell me you only locked me in here for a minute?"

"But . . ." Was I crazy? If my calculator told the date, I might have been able to convince him. But it only told the time. If someone else had been with me or in the house the whole time, I could prove I was telling the truth. But there was only Fred, who was romping in the meadow somewhere.

Then it hit me. The telephone. "Look, Barry, I know it sounds crazy, it *is* crazy, but I was really only gone for less than—"

He groaned and rolled his eyes.

"—less than a minute. So let's go back to the house and call the operator and find out what the date is, okay?"

He didn't say anything, but at least he was beginning to look a little puzzled instead of angry.

"You'll believe the operator, won't you?"

"Yeah, sure," he said, pulling on his pants. "At least then you'll have to stop making your dumb excuses."

In the kitchen I plucked the receiver from the old black wall phone. "We flew out here on August 5, right?" I said.

"Uh huh. And the next morning, the sixth, you locked me inside that place, all day and night, and today you let me out. Today's the seventh."

"And I say I only left you there for a minute, so today's the sixth." I dialed and leaned toward him, holding the earpiece so that we could both hear.

"Can I help you?" said the singsong voice.

"Yes," I said, expecting one of those chatty small-town operators from the movies. "Could you please tell me what the date is today?"

There was a moment of silence. "It is not our job to supply that type of information," she said.

I couldn't get anything else out of her. Directory Assistance was no help either. I felt like screaming at them.

"*Now* will you give up?" Barry said. He stalked over to the cabinet and grabbed a bag of potato chips and began shoving them into his mouth. "Those survival biscuits are lousy, by the way," he said, with his mouth full.

I sank down at the table and rested my head on my arms. Maybe I really was crazy.

"Yoo-hoo, anybody home?" called a female voice. The back door rattled.

"Come in!" I called out. I felt shy around Lucy, but I couldn't have been happier to see her now. I jumped up from the table.

She let the screen door slam and strolled into the kitchen. "Hi," she said casually to Barry, hardly even looking at me. "I left my towel here. Had to come back and get it before Ma noticed. Then I thought, long as it's here, maybe we could go for a swim." She looked at me, then back to Barry. "Something wrong?" she asked him.

He was still furious, and wanted to get back at me. But I could feel how embarassed he was about the crazy thing I had done and how he didn't want to say anything to her about it. If his twin brother was nuts, what did that mean about him?

"No, nothing's wrong," he said. "Just having a little brotherly disagreement. Sure, I'd love to go for a swim. But I don't think Harry wants to. Do you, Harry?"

He was telling me not to come along and daring me to disobey him. "Oh, that's *your* towel," I said. "*When* did you leave it here?"

"Huh?" She shrugged and grimaced as if there were something wrong with me. "I left it here last night. When else was I here?"

"Last night, before we went into the playhouse, right?" I pressed her.

"What about it?" she said, picking up the towel and not even trying to hide the questioning look she shot at Barry.

Barry was staring at her, a handful of potato chips halfway to his mouth. "Night before last, you mean," he said.

"I mean last night," she said, frowning at Barry now, as if he were peculiar too. "When I came over, and you showed me around, and we went inside the playhouse."

"That was *last* night?" Barry said. It was finally beginning to sink in.

"There *is* something the matter," she said, edging away. "Maybe I better go."

"You told her to say it was last night!" Barry accused me, flinging the potato chips to the floor. "You bribed her or something!"

"Bribed me? But I ain't *seen* him since last night when we were all three out there by—" She looked back and forth between us, her mouth half-open. She was probably thinking we were both as crazy as old man Kittery.

"Last night?" Barry asked me. "She's not kidding?"

"You were in there for less than a minute, Barry," I told him. But I knew that Barry wasn't making up what had happened to him. I was beginning to realize what his experience in the playhouse had to mean. It seemed impossible—yet it had happened. I was scared, but at least now Barry knew that I wasn't crazy.

"You left me in there today, for less than a minute," he said slowly. "But to me, it was..." He actually began to smile. "Harry, does this mean what I *think* it does?"

I nodded. "Time goes faster in there," I said.

☐

7

I wouldn't let Barry experiment with my calculator, but I remembered that Mom had packed a battery-operated travel clock for us which we hadn't bothered to take out of the suitcase. It only took Barry a moment to find it. Then the three of us were hurrying across the meadow.

Lucy still thought we were crazy. But Barry's excitement was catching, and she couldn't resist coming with us. "You trying to tell me you were in there for a few seconds, and you thought a whole day and night went by?" She laughed, trotting along beside Barry.

"That's right." Barry was still smiling.

"He's putting us on, ain't he?" she said to me.

"Wait'll you see how clean the place is," Barry said. "That took at least five hours. And I fell asleep. And my beard grew. That couldn't all happen in less than a minute."

"How do I know your beard grew?"

"He shaved this morning," I told her.

"I don't get it."

"Time goes faster in there; it's the only explanation," I said.

"Time goes faster? What's that supposed to mean?"

We passed the sundial. "It's like . . . Think of it like that river," I said. "The pool where you went swimming—the water hardly moves at all. But in another place, where it's shallow and the riverbed slopes, the water moves faster there." We stopped at the door. "This playhouse, or maybe the rock it's built on, is like the rapids in a river. Time goes faster here."

"You just fell asleep," she said to Barry.

"Never read any science fiction, did you?" Barry asked her, unlocking the door.

She pursed her lips into the sardonic grimace that was beginning to seem familiar. "Sure didn't. And I won't start if that's the kind of cuckoo ideas it gives you."

Barry remained on the threshold, holding the door open. "Cuckoo ideas, huh?" he said. "I'll show you how cuckoo. See this clock? Nothing wrong with it? It's telling the right time?" He offered it to her like a magician asking a member of the audience to examine his top hat.

"Sure, you just set it five minutes ago," she said. "Yeah, it looks okay."

Barry, meanwhile, rushed inside and with one lightning movement propped open the door, which opened inward, with the metal chair. "Okay," he said, jumping out. "Everybody can see in now?"

We nodded. I had my calculator in my hand.

"Well, look closely."

He sat the clock down on the stone slab, just inside the door.

For five seconds or so the clock ticked along normally. Then, as we watched, it began to go faster. The second hand spun around wildly and then vanished into a blur. The minute hand raced after it. In a moment it was a blur as well, like a pale film over the clock face. But we could still see the fat hour hand, jerking visibly from one hour to the next, and getting faster. Its motion was halting and uneven, as though it were trying to resist but couldn't. As it approached the speed of a second hand, it began to quiver. There was a ratchety whining noise. The clock trembled, and the blur was gone. The second and minute hands, twisted together, came to a grinding halt. The hour hand, disconnected from the mechanism, swung between five and seven, gradually losing momentum.

Barry snatched the clock back and shook it. The insides rattled. "Couldn't take the pace," he said. He looked back inside the playhouse. "It's not just any rapids in there—it's a regular Niagara Falls."

"It was ticking off the hours exactly as fast as seconds, right before it broke, I said, switching off the calculator. "Incredible."

"Sure is," said Lucy. "Time going faster!" She snorted. "No little trick clock's gonna make me believe *that*!"

"You think the clock was fixed?" Barry asked her.

"What else? You coulda got it in a joke store."

Barry shrugged. "Fine, believe anything you want." He tossed the ruined clock in his hand. "Too bad.

56

Now you'll never know what happened to your grandpa's animals."

"Huh?" she said.

"Hey, Harry, I'm starving," he said, "Let's have some lunch. We got all kinds of exciting plans to make. This is going to be the greatest two weeks of my whole life!"

"Sure," I said numbly. I knew there had been nothing funny about that clock. Time went faster in the playhouse—there was no other explanation. But unlike Barry, I didn't see the possibilities as thrilling. To me, the playhouse seemed about as much fun as an unexploded bomb.

Lucy, despite her skepticism, came along with us—as Barry wanted her to. He wasn't interested in making plans with just me. "What did you mean about Grandpa's animals?" she asked Barry.

"I know what happened to them now."

I looked around for Fred again as we approached the house. I hadn't seen him since breakfast and was beginning to wonder if he might have gotten lost.

"Yeah?" Lucy was saying as we went inside. "What happened to them?"

"They starved to death—like I'm about to. What have we got, Harry?"

"The usual. Tuna fish. Peanut butter and jelly."

"Peanut butter and jelly. You make them better than me."

"You want one, Lucy?"

"All right, thanks," Lucy said, sitting down at the table across from Barry. "What do you mean, they starved to death?"

"They got onto that rock, where time goes faster. And it goes a lot faster—an hour for every second outside." I heard him shaking the ruined clock again. "Same thing happened to all the little skeletons. A few minutes went by, outside. But it was days and days to them. They starved. And after they died, they'd rot and decompose just as fast."

"Yeah, but—"

"Think of all the dead insects, and the spiderwebs. It's been *centuries* in there since Uncle Ambrose died."

"Yeah, but back in Grandpa's day, there wasn't no playhouse to lock the animals in. Why didn't they just leave when they got hungry?"

"I don't know. Maybe something held them there. Maybe Uncle Ambrose kept them there somehow."

"But *why*?"

"He must have noticed peculiar things about that rock. Maybe he was doing experiments, trying to figure it out. I'd like to do a few experiments myself." He thought for a moment. "That pump out in back of the playhouse must be rigged up to supply a huge amount of water instantly. And he needed all those batteries for the light, because if he used the regular power company, his bill would have been gigantic."

There was a loud jangling sound. I jumped and dropped a glob of peanut butter on the floor.

"Hello," Barry said, quickly answering the phone. "Oh, hi, Mom."

I hurried over to stand beside him. "Let me talk to

her," I whispered. I knew I missed her more than he did.

"What do you mean, who is it? It's *me*, Barry, Mom." He scowled and shrugged me aside. "Yeah, everything's fine... *He's* fine too."

I hovered impatiently beside his chair, eager to get on the phone and tell her my own version of what it was like here.

"Yeah, there's lots of stuff that might be worth something. Doesn't seem like there's been any vandalism...What's that?..." He smiled, then turned and looked up at me, holding my eyes as he said slowly, "No. Nothing peculiar at all."

He didn't want me to say a word about the playhouse. And what would happen if I did? Mom wouldn't understand what I was talking about. But she *would* think I'd gone nuts. She'd cancel her trip and come to Sushan as fast as possible, maybe even today. And that might interfere with whatever "adventures" or experiments Barry was planning.

"But what about you? What've you been doing?" Barry asked her, still watching me. He was putting off the moment when I'd get on the phone.

But I didn't care. It would be so easy. All I'd have to do was tell her, and she'd be on her way.

"Come on, Barry," I said, reaching for the phone.

He pressed the phone against his ear and shook his head at me. "Uh huh. Sounds wonderful."

Then I began to wonder—would it really be that simple if I told her? First of all, she'd be hysterical at my craziness. It would ruin her vacation. And even if she did get a flight today, there would still be many hours before she arrived at the house—hours during which Barry would be furious. There would be terrible fights, and I hated fighting—not to mention that Barry would make me feel like such a mama's boy in front of Lucy. Perhaps telling Mom would only make everything worse.

"I'll get him." He took the phone from his ear. "Harrrry!" he called, as if I were in another room. He held the phone in his lap with one hand over the mouthpiece. He glared at me, his mouth set in a hard line. He handed me the phone.

"Hi, Mom," I said. Barry didn't take his eyes from me. "Yeah . . . yeah, sure, everything's fine."

Barry relaxed, and turned back to Lucy, who was looking back and forth between us curiously.

"The lawyer guy was okay. . . . Yeah, there's plenty of food here. We're just having lunch. . . . Peanut butter and jelly sandwiches . . . Last night I made grilled cheese and tomato soup. . . . Okay, I'll say hi to Fred. He's having a great—" My voice suddenly stopped.

"Yes? What about Fred?" Mom said.

Barry had turned back to me again.

"Harry? Harry, are you there? What's the matter?" Mom said.

"Nothing . . . nothing at all. Uh . . . Fred's having a great time. He loves the country. Chasing rabbits and things."

Barry nodded, smiling tightly at me. A moment later Mom said good-bye and hung up.

"Very good, Harry," Barry said.

Lucy looked puzzled. "You two sure are the *strangest* pair of—"

"The playhouse door," I said, the receiver still in my hand. "You left the chair there. It's still open, isn't it."

"Did I?" Barry shrugged. "So what? You finish those sandwiches yet?"

"Fred," I said. And I dropped the receiver and ran for the door.

8

"Fred!" I shouted as I ran. "Here, boy! Here I am, Fred. Don't go in there, Fred. Please, Fred. Here, boy!"

The playhouse door was closed, and locked. For a moment I felt a flood of relief—Barry had taken away the chair after all. Then another possibility occurred to me. I turned back to run for the keys. I almost bumped into Barry and Lucy.

"The keys! Did you bring the keys?"

"Yeah, I have them," Barry said, just standing there.

"Open it! Hurry!" I screamed.

"Okay, okay, calm down," Barry said.

"Did you leave it open or not? Can't you remember?"

"I . . . I think it was open," Lucy said, sounding scared.

Barry opened the door. I pushed past him. Then I moaned and sank to my knees. The playhouse went dark as the door slammed behind the three of us, and I had the futile hope that I hadn't really seen what I thought. But a second later Barry turned on the light, and there it was again.

The pile of bones at the foot of the bed was not immediately recognizable and could possibly have been some other animal. It was the metal chain and dog tag lying among the bones on the stone floor that made the identification absolute. I closed my eyes. I felt the tears spring up and trickle down my cheeks, but I made no attempt to stop them or even hide them. It didn't matter what the others thought of me. Nothing mattered except Fred.

I heard the scrape of metal as Barry picked up the chair and the click of the door as they went out. I was glad they were gone. Part of me knew I was now locked inside and that it could be dangerous, but I didn't care. All I cared about was Fred.

I thought about Fred as a puppy, about Fred waiting eagerly for me to come home from school, about Fred careening through the meadow, his long ears catching on things. I tried hard not to think about what it had been like for Fred to be trapped in here, getting hungry, getting weak, barking and whimpering and crying to be let out, and no one coming to help him for days and days. I didn't think at all about how much time was going by, or what that meant.

And what had happened to Fred was Barry's fault.

Eventually my knees got stiff and sore, and my feet kept falling asleep, and my eyes and throat began to ache from crying. I stood up and looked blearily around the small room. There were some other thin bones scattered about on the floor and more cobwebs. I sat down on the bed. I saw then that I wasn't locked in after all. Barry had left the keys on the table, so that I'd be able to get out whenever I wanted. It was a thoughtful gesture, but irrelevant. I couldn't forgive him for what had happened to Fred. At least, after this, he would see that the playhouse was too dangerous to fool around with. He would *have* to agree that the best thing to do was lock it up and stay away from it.

Or would he?

The more I brooded about it, the more convinced I was that Barry wouldn't see it my way. He would be upset about Fred, but he'd still be fascinated by the playhouse. And arguing with him wouldn't make any difference—his curiosity and appetite for adventure were too strong to be affected by logic. Not until we went home, and it was physically impossible for him to get to the playhouse, would Barry leave it alone.

My eyes fell on the keys. And I knew what I had to do.

Before, I wouldn't have had the guts to consider it. Even now, after Fred, I knew that Barry would not forgive me for it. But I didn't care. I hadn't forgiven him either. With the playhouse keys at the bottom of the river, we'd be safe from it. And maybe that would make up, in a small way, for what had happened to Fred.

But I had to act, not sit around thinking about it. I knew myself well enough to see that I must do it fast, before I lost my nerve. And now I had a chance. Barry had been hungry; they were probably back at the house eating. I'd be able to dash down to the river and dispose of the keys without anybody trying to stop me. And then everything would be solved.

I turned the keys in the lock, pulled open the door and rushed out.

And plunged into a life-sized photograph, a still frame from a movie.

Barry and Lucy were poised at the playhouse door. One of Barry's feet was lifted, caught in midstep. His mouth stretched open, his tongue slightly curled and immobile between his upper and lower teeth. Lucy faced him, a single tear, solid as a transparent glass bead, affixed to her cheek.

There was dead silence. A large white butterfly hung motionless in the air a foot above Lucy's head.

Only I was moving, with such momentum that I couldn't stop myself. I lurched between Barry and Lucy, bruising my shoulders as I scraped against their stonelike bodies. My foot caught in the threshold and I tumbled forward onto the grass. I rolled over.

Barry and Lucy slowly began to bend, pushed apart by the impact of my body. They tipped away from each other, millimeter by millimeter, like a film gradually speeding up. The butterfly crept forward, its wings moving with sluggish deliberateness as though it were trapped in molasses. Behind them, foliage blinked and shivered. There was a whooshing sound, like air filling a vacuum container. It became a gravelly rumble, rapidly rising in pitch, taking on more voices, a racing scream of wind and insects and water. Barry and Lucy's faces melted into expressions of shock as they neared the ground.

They landed. The playhouse door slammed shut. The butterfly dipped and sailed away. The noisy crescendo stabilized into the muted buzzing murmur of a summer day.

"Huh?" Barry said, sitting up and rubbing his shoulder. "Where'd *you* come from?"

Lucy could only stare at me.

"You just sprang up out of *nowhere!*" Barry said, beginning to get to his feet.

I had forgotten what I was doing. If I hadn't just sat there gaping stupidly at the world coming to life, I could have had a head start. And I needed one, because Barry can run faster than me. It was probably already too late.

Then I thought of Fred. I sprang up and dashed out of the circle of trees. Barry was stunned. Maybe I had a chance.

I fled past the sundial. I heard a startled shout behind me and then footsteps thudding on the hard earth. But I didn't slow myself down by turning back to look. I ran for the underbrush and the trees.

"Hey! Wait! Where you going with those keys?"

They were still dangling from my hand. Barry knew what I was doing. I had to get them in the water before he caught me. I tore through the junglelike underbrush and slipped and skidded down the slope.

I had reached the fast, shallow part of the river where the bottom was visible. I wanted the slow, dark pool, where the keys would be irretrievably lost. I stumbled along the stony bank, gasping. I could hear the crunch of gravel as Barry closed in on me.

I would never make the pool. I threw the keys into the noisy water.

Then I was pushed violently from behind. I tumbled forward, my hands in the river. Barry splashed past me. He waded out to the middle, sliding on the slippery rocks. He fell to his knees, not thinking about getting drenched, and ran his hands over the bottom. The water there was about an inch deep. In a moment he turned toward me, still sitting in the water, and held up both keys.

I had managed to keep my shirt from getting wet, and was standing on the bank. Lucy came trotting up beside me. I didn't want to look at her. I felt foolish, and I wanted Fred back. Everything was awful.

Barry stood up in the water. "Don't do that again," he said calmly. He wasn't out of breath at all. He put the keys in his mouth, peeled off his sopping T-shirt, balled it up and threw it to the bank. He untied his sneakers and kicked them after the shirt. He buttoned the playhouse keys into the back pocket of his running shorts. He put his hand on his hips. "How about that swim?" he said.

Lucy was staring at him. Barry and I have the same plump-cheeked face, the same small nose and rounded chin, and we're the same height. But Barry is an athlete, and I hate sports. His body is lean and hard, and I'm a little soft. I could tell by the way Lucy watched him that she was impressed by his body. Barry knew it too.

She turned toward me. "You... want to go in?"

I shook my head. How could Barry even *think* of going swimming now?

"I'm sorry about your dog," she said shyly. At least she seemed uncomfortable about going swimming right after Fred had died. But she couldn't resist Barry. "I got my suit on underneath," she called back to him. Then, turning away from me with a guilty expression, she began taking off her shoes.

I left them and walked back to the house, staying well away from the circle of trees around the playhouse. In the kitchen, I saw Fred's feeding bowls and almost started crying again. I still needed to take some kind of action. Barry had squelched me over the playhouse keys as he always squelched me. Wasn't there anything I could do?

My eyes fell on the house keys, hanging on a hook over the table. I thought of the locked attic and the locked metal box where we had found the first playhouse key. I took the keys and went upstairs.

Inside the box were four books, a small bundle of letters tied with string and a leather-bound volume that seemed to be a diary. I locked the empty box and took its contents down to my room.

I hated the playhouse, I was terrified of it, but I also couldn't help being curious. It had only been a few minutes ago that I had come rushing out of it into the strangest experience of my life. Maybe if I understood a little more about it, I wouldn't be so afraid.

I examined the contents of the box. There was nothing ominous about the books, which seemed to be physics texts, full of formulas. I flipped through them quickly and then put them on the floor. The letters were from university professors. Maybe later I would study them, but at the moment I was too keyed up. I put them with the books and opened the leatherbound volume.

It was a diary, hastily scrawled in pencil. The first date seemed to be May 6, 1919. I flipped through it quickly, to see how recently Uncle Ambrose had last written in it. Toward the end, the handwriting deteriorated. The last entry was dated this year, but had no month or day. It was practically illegible, the letters half-formed, obscured by smudges. But I wanted to know the last thing he had written. I persevered. And after about ten minutes, I thought I had it. The entry read:

Today I saw... It progresses. Afraid... Remember the other one. Hope walls strong enough... keep It from getting out.

9

The double keys, the walls that seemed too strongly built for such a small structure. We had assumed that their function was to keep animals, and people too, from getting inside the playhouse and onto the rock. But we had been wrong.

Their real function was to keep something— something referred to as It by Uncle Ambrose—from getting out.

I closed the diary and dropped it on the other stuff. I lay down on the bed, curled up as if I were cold and tried not to think.

The playhouse was a menace. Other people—the lawyer, the police—had to be warned about it. Then it would be their problem.

But this time I wouldn't be hysterical. I'd wait until Barry and Lucy came back, and then I would calmly show the diary to them. And then they would see that I wasn't such a sissy after all.

It wasn't long before I heard them in the kitchen, ravenous after their swim. I gave them a few minutes to make sandwiches and eat, and then I brought down the books, the letters and the diary. I put them on the table and sat down. "Have a good swim?"

"Uh huh," Barry said, swallowing. "And don't get your hopes up—I didn't lose the keys. What's all that?"

"The stuff from the box in the attic."

"Oh, that. I forgot about it. This stuff was locked in a box with one of the keys," he told Lucy. He pushed the end of his sandwich into his mouth. "Anything interesting?"

"This. It's Uncle Ambrose's diary." I opened it and set it in front of him. "Just read this last entry."

In the end, I had to decipher it for them. Barry was skeptical. "'It progresses. . . . keep It from getting out,'" he said. "But what *is* It?" He was more irritated than frightened. "This doesn't make sense."

"I don't know what It is, but It must be pretty bad for him to make that special door and steel walls to keep It in," I said.

"Maybe It's something that ate your dog—and my grandpa's animals too," Lucy said, looking worried. "Maybe we better tell somebody."

"I think that's a good—"

"But nothing ate them—they starved to death," Barry interrupted. "Fred did, for sure. His bones were all in the right places. If something ate him, they would have been scattered all around—like the bones of whatever it was that Fred chased in there."

"Maybe it's something that eats...differently." I said.

"But there isn't anything in there!" Barry shouted. "I was in there longer than anybody, and I know there wasn't anything else. Uncle Ambrose just got confused in his old age, that's all. Or else you're reading it wrong."

"We should read the rest of the diary, then, and see what else he says."

Barry looked at it again. "Be my guest," he said, pushing the diary back at me. "It took fifteen minutes to figure out what that one sentence *might* say, and the rest of it is just as bad. It'll take forever." He reached for the little bundle of correspondence.

I glanced through the diary again. Barry was right. Even most of the dates were difficult to make out. I began to feel a little frantic. I had been so sure that they would be convinced by the diary. But Barry was making it seem as though I were just being hysterical again. And the more I protested, the more stupid he would make me feel in front of Lucy. It was the same predicament he was always putting me in—in front of Mom and Dad and kids we knew at home. And it always worked: I gave in, and he got his way.

"At least these are typed," Barry said, looking over the letters. "Listen to this. It's from some college professor. 'Dear Mr. Kittery,'" he read. "'I cannot view with any credibility the phenomena you describe in your letter. I am afraid that you are operating under certain fundamental delusions. I would suggest that you seek the advice of a physician.'" He put the letter at the bottom of the pile and read from another. "'Dear Mr. Kittery, Do not waste my time and yours by sending me another one of your delusional letters. This is the last response you will receive from me.'"

"Almost makes me feel sorry for the old guy," Lucy said, unexpectedly. "That guy thought he was crazy, and everybody around here did too. And all the time, that rock, and the playhouse, really were... There really was something wrong about them... whatever."

"But *what*?" Barry said. "There must be some reason why it... Huh." He looked more closely at the next letter in his hand.

Was I really going to give up this easily? But maybe I *was* just being hysterical. Lucy was a little worried, but she wasn't running to call the police. I wasn't even sure anymore that the diary said what I had thought. And I was getting interested in the letters too. Maybe there was an answer here.

"This one's from another scientist." Barry glanced at the dates. "The letters are in order. Seems like Uncle Ambrose changed his approach. Listen. 'Dear Mr. Kittery, Your theoretical question on the alteration of time is quite imaginative.' See, Uncle Ambrose said it was *theoretical*, so this guy wouldn't think he was a crackpot," Barry explained and went on reading. "'And there are, in fact, two real situations in which the flow of time is altered—during acceleration and in the presence of a gravitational field.'"

Barry turned to Lucy. "This guy's a scientist, and he says it's possible."

"Go on, read it," I said.

"'Time moves more slowly for an accelerating object than a stationary one. This has been proven by experiment. But the change is so infinitesimal that only when an object approaches the speed of light does its time dilation become significant. If an astronaut could travel at almost the speed of light, he might go on a trip that took five hundred years—to an observer on the earth—but the traveler would experience it as lasting for only a year.

"'Unfortunately, with present technology, it is not possible for any ship or any astronaut to approach the speed of light. This time dilation, though real, has only been achieved with subatomic particles.'"

Barry cleared his throat. "'Time also slows down for any object in a gravitational field. But, once again, this effect is so minimal that it becomes noticeable only under the most extreme conditions—such as when an object is in the vicinity of a black hole and the singularity at its core!'"

Now Barry looked up at me. He seemed to have forgotten he was mad at me. "Listen to that, Harry, a *black hole*," he said. "Wow! And what's this about a singularity? You ever heard of that before?"

"Yes."

"What's a black hole?" Lucy said. "I don't like the sound of it."

"Maybe he explains," Barry said, and began reading again. "'A singularity is a star that has died and collapsed in upon itself. Because of the huge gravitational forces, it is reduced to a fraction of its former size. Its vast mass is compressed into a minute volume. Its gravitational pull is so strong that not even light, the fastest thing in the universe, can escape from it—hence the popular name black hole.'"

"That's really true?" said Lucy.

"Uh huh," Barry said. "Listen. 'And so a singularity has a peculiar effect on time.'" He paused. "'Once an object has gotten within a certain radius, known as the event horizon, time slows down almost to the point of stopping. To the object within a singularity's event horizon, one minute goes by—while the rest of the universe experiences hundreds of years. Of course, this is another situation in which no human being is ever likely to find himself.

"'As you see, Mr. Kittery, these are both examples of time being dilated, or slowed down. As for time contracting, or speeding up, which you imagine and describe so wittily—I'm afraid the evidence for that exists only in the most speculative formulae of theoretical physicists.'"

Barry put the letter down. "A lot he knows," he said.

"He does know a lot," I said. "I never knew that a singularity had an event horizon, and inside it, time almost stops." I was pretty good at science, and Barry and I both devoured science fiction. The letter was so intriguing that I almost forgot to be afraid of the playhouse; I almost—but not quite—forgot about Fred. "I think it's all really fascinating," I said.

"Well I think old man Kittery finally found another crackpot to listen to him," Lucy said.

"The guy is a professor, chairman of the physics department at this university," Barry said.

"Singularities—or whatever—are real?" she asked again.

"They think so," I told her. "Off in outer space somewhere."

"Wow!" Barry said, his eyes moving quickly over the last letter. "This is . . . This is far out. . . ."

"Read it! Hurry up!" I demanded.

"'I found your response to my letter extremely interesting,'" Barry read quickly. "'Several of my colleagues did too. In fact, you seem to have stumbled on the only evidence there is for the theoretical concept of time contraction.'"

Barry smiled. "See, there *is* evidence," he said and went on reading. "'Yes, of course we have all heard of the conservation of momentum, the rule that every action has an equal and opposite reaction. And there is certainly logic to your idea that the rule might apply to a singularity—that if time slows down on one side of the singularity, then to balance it, *time would speed up on the other side of the singularity.*'"

Barry stopped and looked at both of us.

"Gee, that kind of does make sense," I said, starting to feel scared again.

"'Time would speed up on the other side of the singularity.'" Barry reread the sentence, then continued with the letter. "'There has been much scientific speculation about what might lie beyond a singularity. All the matter that is sucked into it must go somewhere. There are those who believe that a singularity could be an opening, or hole, connecting to a different universe.

"'If that were true, Mr. Kittery, then perhaps your time contraction field would greet the hypothetical traveler as he emerged from one universe into the other.'"

❑

10

I stayed in the kitchen as the afternoon went by outside the window. I didn't want to look at the diary—it was too hard to read and too close to home. Instead, I got out the calculator and turned to the physics books. A couple of them had been published quite recently and seemed very up to the minute. The formulas were wonderfully distracting, like difficult puzzles, and just what I needed to keep myself from brooding about Fred.

"What's he doin'?" Lucy asked Barry.

"Just working the crazy formulas in those dumb books," Barry said. I was better at math and science than he was, but he always tried to play it down so he wouldn't look like the stupid one.

The two of them roamed restlessly around the house looking for more clues about the playhouse. Every once in a while Lucy would glance at me with a kind of puzzled awe. She seemed surprised that I wasn't a complete dolt. I pretended not to notice.

Though Barry had been skeptical about It progressing, and It getting out, he did not make a move toward the playhouse, and neither did Lucy. Maybe it was just a reluctance to confront Fred's bones again. We knew that if we left them there long enough they would crumble away to dust and be hidden under more insect bodies, and then no one would have to dispose of them. Even I didn't feel like burying them and making a little grave. Fred was gone, nothing would change that. And I didn't want to go back to the playhouse.

Before Lucy went home to supper, Barry urged her not to say anything to her parents, or anyone else. "If other people came poking around, it would spoil all the fun. Then we'd never get the chance to figure out what's happening there ourselves."

"Do we really want to?" she wondered.

"Sure we do! We don't want cops to come and rope it off and keep us from going inside."

"You think they'd do that? Then that means it really is dangerous!"

"No, no," he said hastily. "That's just the kind of thing they always do, to keep kids out."

She turned back to me from the door. "Hey, I just remembered. This afternoon, when you knocked us over. What was that all about?"

I looked up from the calculator. I hadn't noticed how late it was getting. "What did it look like to you?"

"We just came out the door, and then there was a kind of . . . like an explosion." Barry looked at Lucy.

She nodded.

"And we fell down, and then you were there, out of nowhere."

I told them what it had been like for me—the frozen world gradually coming back to life. "It was the *weirdest* thing that ever happened to me," I finished. I glanced back at the book for a long moment, doing my best to look scholarly. "But now I think I'm beginning to understand what was happening."

"What?" they both said.

I paused again, enjoying being the center of attention for a change. "Well, when I was inside the playhouse, I was in a time contraction field, right? I was moving faster in time. Every second in the outside world was an hour to me in there."

"Like what happened to me," Barry said.

Lucy frowned.

"You *still* don't believe it!" Barry cried.

"Just go on," Lucy told me.

"Then I ran out. But my body was still moving faster in time than everything else. It must take a few seconds for a body to slow down to real time—the way it took a few seconds for the clock to speed up."

"Makes sense," Barry said.

"So if you go through the doorway slowly, like we usually do, you don't notice the change. but I went so fast you couldn't see me. And when I did slow down, I was already sitting there, so to you it looked like I appeared out of nowhere. And to me it looked like you were statues."

"I still can't believe it!" Lucy said, and made her disgusted expression. "But..." She sighed. "But I also can't believe you two would go to so much trouble to play a trick on me."

"So you just don't know what to believe, do you?" Barry pressed her.

"Uh uh." She nodded unhappily.

"Well then you shouldn't say anything about it to anyone. They'll just think you're crazy, like they thought Uncle Ambrose was crazy."

"I . . . guess."

"Good girl," Barry said. He slung his arm over her shoulder and walked her out of the room to the back door.

I went back to the physics book. But soon I was sorry I had ever opened it.

The tremor woke me in the middle of the night.

A silent shock wave—a noise that wasn't a noise—shattered my dream about Fred. I jolted upright in the darkness. For a fraction of a second, the earth rocked sickeningly beneath me. It was over so quickly it might never have happened, just a final impulse from my dream.

Then Barry was standing in the doorway. "You feel that?"

"Yeah. It was just a dream." That was what I wanted to believe. And, in fact, Barry and I had gone through a period of sharing dreams—but it had been a long time since Barry would admit it.

And he wouldn't now. "That wasn't any dream. I *felt* something, after I woke up—like a little earthquake. And I sort of heard something too. I bet it came from the playhouse."

"Probably," I said, wide-awake enough now to be terrified.

"Come on," Barry said, dashing from his room. In a second or two he was back with his running shorts on. "Come on, get moving!" He hopped on one leg at a time to pull on his shoes.

"But I *can't*!" I wailed, huddled in bed, "I can't *go* to that place now. Don't make me, please!"

"You want me to go alone?" He approached the bed.

"No, Barry, I don't want you to go. Nobody should go. It's not safe."

He tore the sheet away and flung my jeans at me from the floor. "Hurry up!" he ordered. "Things happen fast there."

"No! You don't know," I whimpered. "You don't know what it said in those books. It's worse than you ever thought."

But at the same time I was slipping on my pants and then reaching for my shoes. I was so scared my skin, covered with goose bumps in this 80-degree night, was twitching as though I had just stepped out of an icy pool. Yet I was going with him.

"Come on, hurry up!"

"But I can't find my shirt."

"You don't need one. It's hot out."

"But—"

"Just come on!"

We hurried out of the room and down the stairs. Why was I doing this? He had certainly been mean enough to me so that he deserved to go alone.

But I didn't want him to go alone. I didn't want to lose him.

He grabbed the flashlight, and we were out the back door. "What did you mean, about those books?"

"It's true, about the singularity. It's theoretical, but it's all based on real data—like singularities absorbing light and things that happen to subatomic particles. They've done experiments where protons actually seem to go *backwards* in time. And there's these things called tachyons that they think might actually—"

"But what about the playhouse?" he said, moving smoothly ahead of me.

"Time slows down on the outside of a singularity, in the event horizon. So it would speed up on the inside, after something got sucked through it. And a singularity can be a hole to another universe. And at first I thought the idea of the playhouse being on the inside of a singularity—*this* side—was crazy, because singularities only exist in outer space. Except..."

"Except what?"

"Except I was wrong. The other side of a singularity is different. It could be anywhere—even on the surface of a planet, even in the middle of a meadow. But the worst part is..." I could barely get the words out.

Barry was at the sundial. He stopped to wait for me. He touched me. "Go on, Harry," he coaxed. "The worst part?"

"The worst part is, that's the only possible cause there *is* for time speeding up. It's crazy, but it's the only scientific explanation. This playhouse—the rock it's built on—*has* to be a singularity. One side is in another universe. This side is in this universe. It leads from over there to right here."

We stood outside the circle of trees, the flashlight pointed at the ground. The lush Illinois sounds were all around us, the wind breathing in the leaves, the rush of water, the scraping insects. They seemed so familiar now, compared to the soundless shock that had wakened us.

"So . . . we can't really go in there, can we?" I said.

"Why not?" Barry said, and started moving the flashlight toward the invisible playhouse door.

There was a noise behind us. We spun around.

Lucy stood in the flashlight beam.

"You!" Barry cried. "Then you felt it too?"

"Oh, those little quakes happen all the time. I just couldn't sleep, and when I saw the flashlight moving around over here, I wanted to see what was going on."

"The playhouse—it's a link to another universe, that's what it has to be from those books," Barry told her as if *he* had read them. "And that quake might have been something coming through."

I had never said exactly that. But he had made the logical connection.

"I don't know what you mean by another universe," Lucy said irritably. "Why can't you just talk normal?"

"Just come on." Barry turned and aimed the light at the playhouse. There didn't seem to be any change. He jerked his head at us, then walked forward, reaching into his pocket for the keys.

I squeezed his arm. "You're not going to open it."

"I'm not?"

"But you'll let it out!"

"Let what out?" Lucy wanted to know.

"The thing that came through."

"I don't believe it," she said.

"Then what are you doing here?"

"I just... I didn't want to miss anything."

Barry turned the first key in the lock and pulled it out. He inserted the second key.

"Barry... Don't!" I begged him.

"How else can we find out what happened?" He clicked the lock and pushed open the door.

Cobwebs lashed out from the doorway and a rain of insect bodies pelted against our legs. Cold wind rushed past us like a blast of air from an open winter window—only it didn't smell like air. It smelled like chemicals, and like a dissecting room, and like things I had never smelled before. I might have thrown up, but it was over in a second. The door slammed and the cobwebs fluttered back against it.

"Was that something... getting out?" Lucy said, unclasping her arms from Barry's waist.

I let go of his shoulders. My heart was pumping like crazy. "It could have been—except I didn't feel anything solid."

"It was just a blast of gas," Barry said, unlocking the door again. "From all the things that have died in there."

"Methane," I told him.

"I know that. That's what it was, I bet. Don't know why it didn't happen before, though." He pushed the

85

door open, brushed the cobwebs aside, and stepped in. He propped the door open with the chair. Lucy followed him.

"Well, Harry?" Barry said.

I didn't want to be left outside by myself. I stepped over the threshold.

Barry turned on the light. The bones, as I had hoped, were gone.

"Everything's the same," Barry said. "It's getting dirty again, but that happens all the time."

"Look on the floor," I said.

There was something lying just in front of the sink, something that had not been there before.

"Don't touch it!" I shouted as Barry reached for it.

He drew back his hand.

Lucy, her fingers in her mouth, was positioned, as I was, to flee through the open door.

"Why not?" Barry said, squatting by the object on the floor.

"It might be radioactive or have acid on it or poison or something. It might burn you."

Barry grabbed one of the survival biscuit wrappers and dropped it over the thing. Nothing happened. He picked up the paper and examined it. It was unchanged. He prodded the object with his shoe. "Doesn't feel hot or anything."

"We should lock it up and call the police," I said.

"Sure. And they'll never let us get near this place again." Barry reached slowly toward the thing and then brushed it for an instant with one finger. He let his finger rest on it for a few seconds longer. Then, gingerly, he grasped it in his hand and stood up.

I waited, my eyes shielded, ready to duck in case there was an explosion. Nothing happened. And finally I couldn't go on ignoring Barry's muted exclamations of amazement. I moved toward him to get a better look. Lucy followed.

It fit easily in Barry's hand and looked like a cross between a light bulb and a wad of gum. It was whitish and faintly translucent, and glassy, like a bulb. Only it was pimpled with bulges and ridges and deep convolutions. It was startlingly foreign, yet it also made me think of something I knew, something like—

"A brain!" I said. "It looks like a little brain, made of glass."

"I know it does!" Barry snapped.

"But where'd it come from?" Lucy said.

"From . . . the universe on the other side," I said.

She snorted, and looked up at the ceiling. The trapdoor was open. "That's it," she said. "The trapdoor opened when the earthquake hit, and it fell through."

Then Barry shouted and dropped it. We all sprang back.

"Did it burn you?"

"No." He squatted down beside the object again. "I didn't feel anything. But something happened to it." He picked it up and stood up again. "Look at that."

Something was going on inside it. Pinpoints of light flowed along the ridges and convolutions, moving slowly, then speeding up, then moving slowly

87

again, blinking on and off, then somehow diving into the center.

"Ever see anything like that in a joke store?" Barry asked Lucy.

She ignored his gibe. "It's not alive is it?"

"It's not warm," Barry said. "It's not breathing. It's not trying to fight or to protect itself. It's just blinking."

I had been watching the little pinpoints of light. "I think," I said, "I think maybe it's trying to tell us something."

11

"Trying to talk to us?" Barry said. "Then you do think it's alive." He quickly set it down on the table.

"I don't know. But it seems like a machine. I think . . . it could be repeating a pattern. Like a recording, or a message. Something like that plaque they sent into outer space—that shows what people look like and where the earth is."

"Well it ain't saying nothin' to me," Lucy said.

"Me either—but Harry thinks he knows all the answers," Barry said, walking over to the sink.

I stared down at the object on the table. If there was a pattern to it, it was labyrinthine and complex. Just learning to recognize the beginning and the end would take time. As for deciphering what it might be trying to say—that hardly seemed possible.

I heard water dripping and looked up. Barry was washing his hands under the very slow trickle that fell from the tap into the large black metal basin. He rarely washed his hands without being told. "What are you doing that for?" I asked him.

"Getting the cobwebs off. And also...Well, if it really *is* from another universe, I just thought, you know..."

If he was afraid of contamination, he never should have picked up the alien object or even opened the playhouse after the tremor. But of course I didn't say that. Why fight about it now?

Lucy shook her head. "Well, *I* ain't gonna waste the whole night talking about crazy things like this," she said. "I better go back before it starts to get light."

Barry laughed. "I wouldn't worry about wasting time in here. It's going to be months before it gets light outside. Hang around and see, if you don't believe me." He turned off the faucet.

"Look," I said. I picked up the flashlight and directed the beam out through the open door. Another rabbit sat alertly under the sundial, staring at us. "See? Everything's frozen out there."

"Sometimes rabbits do that when they're scared," she said drily. "Watch this." She picked up one of the survival biscuits, bent sideways and swung her arm a couple of times, and then pitched it expertly at the rabbit. She threw like a boy. The biscuit whizzed out the door.

Then it slowed as though moving through water and stopped, hanging in midair. The rabbit didn't move or blink.

"It's going to be a while before it gets to him," I said.

"No!" Lucy said. The color drained from her face.

There was no need for me to be nasty and say "I

told you so." I just kept the light on the suspended biscuit in its olive green wrapper. The clock, perhaps, could have been fixed. But there was only one explanation for what was happening now. It was the first direct evidence she had seen, and I almost felt sorry for her. She seemed close to tears.

"But it can't..."

Barry was being awfully quiet, I suddenly noticed. I turned around. He stood with his hands on the edge of the sink, staring down into it, as still as the rabbit outside. The only thing that moved was the shadow of his head, swaying gently on the ceiling.

"Barry?" I said, feeling my stomach go cold. "Barry? What's the matter?"

Lucy turned around. I switched off the flashlight and dropped it on the bed. We both saw the shadow of his head above us, rippling against a bluish halo. It was eerie, like being inside one of those "What's wrong with this picture?" puzzles. The flaw was so easy to see. The light bulb was on the ceiling; there shouldn't have been a shadow there. And the light bulb wasn't blue.

"Barry!"

"*Shhh!* Come and look," he whispered. "But walk *soft.*"

I moved reluctantly toward him. "What is it?"

"*Shhh!*" he hissed through clenched teeth. "*Be quiet!*"

I bent over the sink and looked inside.

The half inch or so of water against the dark, shiny sink bottom functioned as a kind of mirror, and when I first looked in I could see, on the surface, the shapes of our three heads. But I quickly stopped noticing them because of what was underneath.

The water glowed. It seemed in itself to be a source of light—a pool of liquid neon. It was a rich, luminous blue, like one of those ocean caverns where the only light enters through the water. And it was bottomless. I knew it was only half an inch deep, and yet I felt dizzy looking into it—as though if I fell in, I would go on falling forever.

"Why's the water doing that?" Barry whispered.

"All I can think of is . . . the water's reflecting something, from somewhere, that we can't see," I said.

"Like you can still see the sunset on the ocean after the sun's gone down?"

"Yeah. Except this light . . . It's not sunlight. And that thing there—I don't know what it is."

For the luminous pool wasn't empty. A long shape floated in the radiant haze, vertically suspended. It waited, motionless, fuzzy and indistinct. But we could see that the top part of it was just about to break through the surface.

"Don't touch the sink," Barry whispered. "The smoother the water gets, the better we'll be able to see it."

"But what *is* it?" Lucy asked, sniffling a little.

"Shhh!" Barry hissed furiously.

Two droplets fell into the pool. They were only tears, but the ripples they caused seemed gigantic. The dark thing dissolved into a wavy, shapeless mass.

Barry pushed down the knob between the faucets. The bright bottomless void gurgled away down the drain. We stared at the empty sink bottom. I could feel how scared Barry was—more scared than I had ever known him to be.

Barry was the first to turn away. He picked up the flashlight and aimed it out the door. "Look," he said. "The rabbit's starting to see it."

The rabbit had turned its head a fraction of an inch to the side. Its ears were just noticeably tilted back, and its upper body slightly elongated as though it were preparing to leap. The biscuit had crept half an inch closer to it.

Lucy covered her eyes with her hands. "I won't look," she said. "It's not real. I'm dreaming."

I looked down at the thing on the table. The little lights were still coursing along. "You sure it didn't hurt to touch it, Barry?"

"Sure."

I picked it up. It felt as smooth and cold as a piece of glazed ceramic, only much lighter. I held it up to my eyes and watched it.

"Maybe you should go home and get some sleep, Lucy," Barry said.

"But what'll I tell them? It must be almost morning now, and—" Then she gulped.

"You've only been gone as long as it takes you to get over here," Barry explained. "They're still asleep."

She stood up. All her cockiness and skepticism had left her. "I gotta think about all this," she said.

"Just don't tell anybody, okay?"

She nodded and mumbled an assent.

"You want to stay here, Harry?" Barry said.

"No thanks."

Neither of us wanted to watch Lucy step out the

door and freeze. We left the playhouse together. The door slammed behind us. In the flashlight beam, the rabbit melted and took off. The survival biscuit hit the base of the sundial.

"Nice aim," Barry said.

Lucy smiled. "I pitch on the softball team," she said. "See you."

Barry and I walked back to the house. In the darkness, the object looked like a swarm of tiny, busy fireflies.

"You think the earthquake was that little thing coming through?" Barry asked me.

"Well, it must cause some kind of a shock when anything takes up space that was empty before, pushing the air away and all," I said. "Like a sonic boom. And remember, it just escaped from the event horizon, too."

"Oh?" he said, sounding a little unsure.

"Anything passing through a singularity would have to go through the event horizon first, however many eons it takes. It would have been frozen in time. What we saw in the water—I think it must be a reflection from the other universe. It's kind of a window, looking right into the event horizon."

"Mmm," Barry said as we walked into the kitchen. "Hey, look out for the table, klutz."

I was watching the object in my hand and hadn't been looking where I was going.

"You were too chicken to go in there, and now you can't stop looking at that thing," Barry said.

"It probably *is* dangerous," I said. "But I kind of like it."

Barry gripped my arm, startling me. "That object we saw reflected in the sink," he said.

"Yeah?"

"You think it was something else . . . on its way through the gate?"

I stared at him. "We didn't imagine it."

"No." He stepped away and we started up the dark stairs.

"This is probably a machine," I said. "It was just ahead of that other thing that's still in the event horizon." I stopped on the landing. "That other thing that's coming through next—I wonder if it could be alive?"

12

I didn't sleep much more that night. I put the object on the table by the bed and lay there in the dark watching the lights blink and swirl. I thought about the playhouse, and I thought about Fred and Barry and me and Lucy. And I watched the lights.

Was there a pattern? After a while I began to be aware that the lights were not all the same color. The difference was so slight that I hadn't noticed at first. Even now, in the dark room, I had to concentrate to be able to tell which lights were vaguely greenish, and which yellowish, and which were just white. But to a creature who lived near a star that was not the sun, whose eyes were used to a different spectrum, the colors might be striking.

I kept watching it, getting a little drowsy. Each different color had its own pattern, it seemed, independent of the others. The greens went the fastest, the yellows a little slower and the whites slower still, hardly changing at all. I drifted off to sleep, and when I woke up, the first thing I noticed was that the white pattern had changed.

It was still dark out. A part of me continued to worry that the object might be a bomb that was going to blow up at any minute. Yet my logical side told me it didn't seem like a bomb. This thing seemed like a device for transmitting information. But what were the lights trying to tell me? Perhaps it was a message, something like: "Greetings. This device has been sent ahead to inform you of a visit from another universe." If it were something like that, then I had no hope at all of being able to translate it. But I also suspected the object wasn't that complicated. Something about the pattern gnawed at me. What did it remind me of?

Maybe it wasn't a communication device after all. Maybe it *was* a bomb, and the lights indicated when it was going to go off.

I sighed and turned away from it, hoping to drift off to sleep again. And I must have fallen asleep, because when I woke up the sluggish white lights were in quite a different formation than before.

Then I knew what the object was trying to tell me. The sudden mixture of disappointment and relief was so unexpected that I actually laughed.

Barry, who had almost finished his bowl of cornflakes, didn't laugh when I told him. "A clock!" He scowled up at me from the table. "That's a stupid idea!"

"I thought so too, but it's true." I showed him the different colored lights. "They're like hours and minutes and seconds, though they're probably different lengths than ours."

"How do you set it, then?"

"I haven't figured that out yet, but I will."

I found a clean bowl and filled it with cereal. We were beginning to run out of dishes. We hadn't washed any since we'd been here; dirty ones filled up the sink. "Maybe we should wash the dishes today," I said to Barry as he was on his way out of the kitchen.

"Not me," he said. "Nobody's checking up on us. Why waste any time on that until just before Mom and Dad get here?"

"It's just that . . . the mess will be so bad by then. And it might stink, and attract bugs."

"Go ahead and wash them if you want, like a good little boy. But I'm not doing it until I have to." He thumped upstairs.

I finished my cereal and put the dirty bowl on a pile in the sink. Then I sat at the table and worked on the clock, which kept me from thinking about Fred, and from worrying, and from feeling guilty about the dishes.

"If it was a clock, it would have gone faster when it was inside the playhouse," Barry said, coming downstairs a half hour later. "But those lights *weren't* going any faster in there."

"Of course not," I told him. "Because *we* were in there with it, going just as fast. The only way we'd see any difference is if we were outside and the clock was inside. You know that, Barry."

"Don't tell me what I already know!" It was a good

thing Lucy wasn't there, or he would have been really angry. "Let's go do it, then," he goaded me. "Let's go test it out right now."

A dull thud slammed through my head, and the earth trembled.

A moment later Barry was poised at the door. "Come on. Let's see what it is this time."

He recovered much faster than I did. The shock made me a little disoriented. "You felt that too, like before?"

"Yeah. Come on. Don't you want to see what it is?"

This new arrival must be the thing we had seen last night, floating in the blue haze of the event horizon. The thing I had thought might be alive.

"What's the matter, Harry? What are you afraid of? It's probably just another *clock* or something," he said sarcastically.

"I know I'm right," I said, getting up. "We can prove it when we get there."

"If we ever *do* get there! Will you please hurry up?"

"But what if it's something alive?" I wondered aloud as we ran across the meadow.

"I thought you said anything that came through had to go through the event horizon first, and that would take eons."

"It would."

"Well, you can stop worrying about any creatures then," he told me. "Nothing could live that long. I'm surprised that thing—whatever it is—still works."

"No, no, it would take eons for the rest of the

universe, but not for the thing in the event horizon. That's the whole point. Time stops in there. It might seem like only a few minutes, or hours, to the thing coming through. I bet something *could* live through it."

Again there was a blast of evil-smelling gas, a pelting of insect bodies. Barry propped open the door and turned on the light. Nothing bizarre greeted us. We hurried to the spot on the floor near the sink.

"Sure doesn't *seem* to be alive," Barry said, sinking to his knees.

I relaxed a little and knelt beside him. The object was green, about the size of a fat rubber band, and fuzzy. It seemed to be made up of many thin fibers matted together.

Barry poked it tentatively. It gave a little. He pressed it harder.

"Careful! Don't hurt it."

"If I was hurting it, it would resist," Barry said with hostility. He must have been getting pretty tired of me knowing all the answers.

"What does it feel like?"

"See for yourself." He stood up and wiped off his hand.

It was furry and slightly moist.

"Come on, you're the genius. What is it?" Barry said.

It was not an artifact. But it didn't seem like an animal, either—there was nothing underneath the fibers but more fibers. It was more inexplicable than the clock had been. "I don't have any idea," I said, picking it up with two fingers and depositing it on the table.

I glanced at the frozen world outside the doorway. Lucy was at the edge of the still life, approaching the opening in the trees. She was leaning forward, and the one brown knee I could see was bent as though she was running. "Lucy's out there," I said.

We both watched her for a moment. She made no discernable progress.

"We should go out there and get her," Barry said. "She looks like something's wrong."

"She just heard the earthquake, that's all," I said. I kind of liked being in the playhouse with Barry, cut off from the rest of the world. Why did Lucy have to be included in everything?

"Maybe she'll know what this thing is," he said. "Let's go get her."

"Why should she know? She barely even understands what's happening here."

"Okay, fine. *I'll* go get her, and *you* wait. It should only take about eighteen hours, your time."

I went with him.

She was out of breath and seemed a little startled. She came to a halt just this side of the sundial and approached us cautiously. "Hey, come on, don't *do* that to me," she said, one hand against her chest.

"Do what? We just came out to get you."

"Yeah, but it was like you jumped outta nowhere."

"But otherwise we would have had to wait for you for eighteen hours," Barry explained.

"I swear, I will never get used to this place, *never,*" she said.

"Come on in and see if you know what this thing is."

Barry finally managed to get her to touch it. "Sure, I know. Never seen a green one before, though."

"Well? What is it?"

She shrugged and gestured with one lifted palm. "A hair ball. Ain't you ever seen a hair ball before?"

"*A hair ball!*"

"You know. Like cats throw up. Or like you pull out of a drain. Only why's it green?"

"I don't believe it," I said.

"Sure does look like one," Barry said. The idea amused him.

"But why's it green?" Lucy said again. "Ain't nothin' or nobody that has green hair."

"Not around here. But in another universe they might. I guess..." Barry avoided my eye. "I guess this kind of proves that's where these things are coming from."

"I don't get this other universe stuff," Lucy said. "What is it? Like another planet, with space creatures on it?"

"Yeah, but not just one little planet. It's a whole other *everything*!" Barry spread his arms, grinning at her. "And the connection is right here, in our own backyard. And we're the only ones who know."

"But that's just..." Lucy started to argue. Then she sighed. "Well, I never heard of no animal with green hair on *this* planet." She finally seemed to be accepting the idea. The time contraction field, the scientific proofs, the magical reflection, the alien artifact—none of that had been enough for her. But a hair ball—that was something she could believe in.

I didn't like it. It didn't fit in with the idea that had been forming in my mind of a supertechnological civilization on the other side. A civilization advanced enough to harness the powers of the stars, to reach across space and time to communicate with us. Why would such a civilization send *this* inane object through the gateway?

"How close is this other universe?" Lucy said with an apprehensive glance out the door.

"I don't know, but this is the link," Barry said. "It must be pretty close. We were looking right into it yesterday when we saw that reflection in the sink."

"But then, shouldn't we be careful?" Lucy said. "I mean, maybe we could fall in."

"Fall in..." Barry murmured. Then his eyes lit up, and he whooped and jumped so high his head almost hit the ceiling. "Fall in!" he shouted. "That's it! We *must* be close enough. And maybe, only *inches* from us, there's somebody in their backyard, on the other side, sending things over to us."

"Somebody with green hair—or a green cat," Lucy said.

"Right," Barry said. "And maybe *we* could send something over to them. And then, if that worked— *maybe we could go through ourselves!*"

"No thanks," Lucy said.

"But we could find out first if it was safe," Barry

said. "Just think about it. It would be the greatest adventure *ever*. Compared to *this*, going to the moon would be like walking across the street."

"No, Barry," I said faintly.

"What do you mean, no? Who said *you* had to go? You could stay here and *read* if you're too chicken to come along."

"It doesn't work that way, Barry," I said. "Please don't be mad. It's one-way. It has to be."

"One-way?"

I nodded. "It has to be. You're forgetting what this is, Barry. It's a singularity, a black hole. It sucks up everything that gets close enough—matter, light, everything. There's no escape. Once something falls into the event horizon, it can't communicate with anything else, it can't turn around, it can't go back. It can only go in one direction, toward the center of the singularity. And this is where it ends up."

"How do you know?"

I looked down and didn't even bother to answer him.

"All right, but maybe those books are wrong. Maybe they made a mistake. Maybe we *could* go through."

"Maybe we could—if we found a singularity in *this* universe and got dragged into it. But the one that's making all this stuff happen is in another universe. It sucks things up and deposits them here. They can never go back, and we can never fall into it. It only goes this way."

"You sure?" Lucy asked me.

"I'm sure."

"Well, that's a relief!" she said.

Barry sank down onto the bed. "You don't know everything, Harry," he said. "Sometimes you're not as smart as you think you are."

"Was I right about the other stuff?"

He didn't answer. There was no reason for him to feel humiliated. Lucy liked him better than me—she couldn't have cared less that I knew about science. "Isn't it fantastic enough, just the way it is?" I said. "The time stuff and the things coming through? Anyway, you wouldn't want it to be the other way around."

"Why not?"

"I told you. Think about what it means to go through. Once you start, there's no changing your mind and turning back. And the trip takes so long— even though you don't feel it—that everybody and everything you know would die and disappear. Your own species would probably become extinct, that's how long it takes. You'd be totally alone. And then, if you did get to another universe where you could survive, you'd never be able to go back. You'd be stuck there, the only human being in existence. Think how lonely and awful that would be. You'd... kind of be a singularity yourself."

"Who says that would be so bad?"

"Oh, come on, Barry," I said.

"Hey, let's take a look and see if something else is on the way through," Barry said, standing up quickly and changing the subject. He flipped on the faucet and water trickled into the sink.

It was strange to watch the water begin to glow as it slowly deepened. Barry turned off the faucet. We waited, as the ripples swam back and forth and faded, and the reflected whitish object floating there took on clarity and shape. The reflection worked better with deeper water. The object looked real enough to touch.

But it was impossible to tell what it was. The skin seemed mottled, as though perhaps a network of veins branched across it. There were two dark patches on it, unevenly spaced. The top edge of it, closest to the surface, seemed to have wisps or tendrils protruding from it.

"It's closer than the hair ball was," Barry whispered. "I bet it comes through this afternoon."

Barry soon got tired of watching it float there, and we left the playhouse. Lucy was still amazed that no time had gone by while we had been inside. "This place woulda made a fantastic clubhouse or hideout, wouldn't it?" she said. "You could sneak in here with your friends and play for as long as you wanted. And no one would ever miss you, or try to make you come home, or anything."

"You could still do that," Barry said, watching her.

We tested the brainlike object in the open doorway. The lights did speed up, merging into a constant dull glow.

"That still doesn't prove it's a clock," Barry said.

"When I figure out how to set it, then you'll see."

"Well, I gotta go," Lucy said.

"But it's not nearly lunchtime," Barry told her.

"I know that now. But I still gotta go."

But it felt like lunchtime, and we headed back to the kitchen. I went to the trouble to make B.L.T.'s on toast, a favorite of Barry's. I waited until he had finished, and then I said, "Did you really mean what you said before, about wanting to go through a singularity?"

"What did I say?"

"About how you wouldn't mind saying good-bye to everybody you knew and being the only human there was."

He shrugged. "Who knows? I bet it would be interesting, though."

"It would be awful!"

He looked at me steadily. "Did you ever wonder what it feels like *not* to be a twin?" he asked me.

I felt an unpleasant pang. "No, I guess I never did."

"Well I've thought about that—a lot. To be one of a kind, like most people in the world. Not being stuck with another half. Being on your own. I've always wondered about that," he said, not looking away from me.

I looked away. I'd known for a while that Barry felt this way, but I still didn't like hearing it. This was why, every once in a while, I had the idea that he wanted me to die—it was the only way he could get out of being a twin.

But now, I suddenly saw, there was another way he could escape from twinship. It would be very simple and easy. No one would have to die. No one would have to go anywhere. I grabbed the alien clock and began concentrating on it, thrusting this new idea from my mind—I didn't want Barry to get even the slightest hint of it.

But Barry wasn't stupid. It would only be a matter of time until he figured it out for himself.

And once he did, he could leave me behind for good.

13

The new arrival did come through that afternoon, just as Barry had predicted. It turned out to be a used tissue.

I hated the idea even more than the hair ball. I struggled to find another explanation for it, to believe that it was something else. But I couldn't. My common sense forced me to succumb and accept the inevitable. It was a used alien tissue, and there was nothing I could do about it.

"But why a used tissue? What's the *point*?"

Barry enjoyed my discomfort at the idea. "Maybe there's some powerful germs on it that we have no immunities to," he suggested. "Maybe it'll turn into a plague and wipe out the human race."

"Somebody already wrote that story," I told him. "And anyway, if they were trying to wipe out the human race, they wouldn't do it with an old used tissue."

The clock was the only thing that had come through that wasn't a disappointment, and I was obsessed with it—I was determined to figure out how to set it.

Concentrating on it was also a good way to keep my mind occupied, so that I wouldn't keep thinking about the way Barry could escape from me—and inadvertently pass the idea on to him. I tried to be aware of where he was at all times, to be sure he wouldn't go into the playhouse without me. But I also wanted to keep away from his immediate vicinity, so I wouldn't give anything away. The living room was a good place to keep out of his way. It was so dreary that neither of us wanted to go in there much. But I could also hear everything going on in the house and keep tabs on Barry's whereabouts.

I sat on the uncomfortable couch for hours, not making much progress with the clock. Finally I got restless and began pacing around the room, looking at the neatly mounted skeletons.

And then I remembered. The six-legged cat. The bird-headed snake. Maybe they weren't fakes after all.

So much had happened that we had forgotten all about them. Now I gulped and stared hard at the catlike skeleton. The more I examined it, the more convinced I was that Uncle Ambrose couldn't have faked it. The middle pelvis fit perfectly into the spine, and the ribs around it curved just enough to leave space for it. The middle legs, furthermore, were shaped differently from the forelegs and hind legs, as though their function was slightly different. They couldn't have been lifted from another animal; they belonged there.

I studied the other skeletons in the case now with a more suspicious eye. There was something that looked at first glance like a bird, except that there were three eye sockets in the skull, instead of just two—it wouldn't have had to turn its head from side to side the way earth birds did. The bird-headed snake was just as anatomically flawless as the cat. And I found one we hadn't noticed before, very much like a six-inch-tall monkey—only it had wings and a lizard's long-jawed head.

Barry was furious that I had remembered them before he had. "Who said we both forgot about them?" he bluffed. "*I* didn't."

"Then how come you didn't say anything when we figured out about the singularity and the things coming through from the other universe? That's where these animals must have come from."

"I didn't say anything because . . . I didn't feel like it," he said lamely. "And will you stop nagging me?" He scowled and stamped his foot.

"Careful! You might break them."

"Oh, shut up!"

I turned back to the case and changed the subject. "There are artists at universities and places who can reconstruct what dinosaurs looked like from their skeletons. Wonder what they'd make of these?"

"I'd love to see," he admitted, beginning to be mollified. "I'd love to know what that monkey thing really looked like."

"If we told people about it, we could find out. We really ought to, Barry," I urged him. "We can't just keep this a secret."

"No!" he shouted, angry all over again. "We can't tell anybody. They'll take it all away from us."

I was afraid to argue with him—he might stamp his foot harder and really damage the skeletons. And anyway, I told myself, in a week and a half when Mom and Dad showed up, the rest of the world would have to find out everything. Then we probably would be pushed out of the picture. Barry didn't think it would do any harm to keep it to ourselves for that much longer. Maybe he was right.

"Well, what I want to know," I said, "is did these animals die coming through the gate? Or did they come through alive, and then the atmosphere killed them? Or maybe the atmosphere didn't even kill them. Maybe they came through alive and just starved to death, like the earth animals."

"If that were true," Barry whispered, "Then more of them might still come through—more little bird-headed snakes squirming around. *Wow!*"

"You know what else I wonder?" I said slowly. "I wonder if Uncle Ambrose just might happen to have one of those insect identification books."

"You think all those dead insects might be coming through the gate? Not just crawling in from the meadow and starving?"

"We never really looked at them or tried to see if they were familiar," I pointed out. "And you know how tight that place is."

"The spiders! Maybe the spiders are alien too!"

We started looking on the dining-room table, which was buried in books. "You know what this means," I said, digging through a pile of *National Geographics*. "It means things have been coming through the hole for a while—since before Uncle Ambrose died. Lucy said the quakes happen all the time. We just assumed the clock was the first thing, but it wasn't. There could be more alien objects somewhere in the house!"

"That's right. I bet there's boxes and boxes of used tissues and green hair balls hidden away somewhere," Barry teased me.

"What I meant was artifacts, like the clock," I said.

"But maybe not just artifacts." Barry looked up. "Maybe animals, that got through alive. Or even *intelligent* aliens. Maybe that's what killed Uncle Ambrose. An alien. And now it's lurking around, waiting."

I hadn't thought of that. And I didn't want to. An alien, hiding in the woods somewhere. Or even in the house. We had never been down to the basement, but there had to be one. I squeezed my eyes shut.

"Hey, here it is!" Barry cried.

"What?" I shrieked, jumping up from the table.

"Field Guide to North American Insects," Barry said, laughing at me.

It was evening now. The light slanted lush and golden across the meadow, and the insects' scratchy sighing was like the purr of a gigantic cat—a six-legged one, perhaps.

The silent thud struck when we were just outside the circle of pines. I staggered a little, but I was getting used to it and didn't pause for long. I didn't even try to keep Barry from unlocking the playhouse—not even when he said, "Maybe it's one of those animals; maybe it's still alive!"

Insect bodies rained against our legs. We check the floor before examining them. There was no chirping three-eyed bird or anything else that seemed alive. The new object was a purplish strip, about half an inch wide and six inches long. That curved around on itself in a loose coil. The outer, purplish side of it was just perceptively fuzzy. The inner side was black, with little patches of gooey-looking grayish membrane clinging to it. There was a sharp acidic tang in the air, vaguely reminiscent of turpentine.

"Doesn't look like a tool *or* an animal," I said, disappointed again.

Barry ran his finger along the purple side. "Feel this," he said. "It reminds me of something."

I did so, reluctantly. The sensation was familiar, but I couldn't place it.

"*I* know!" Barry said. "Peach fuzz."

"That's right."

"And the shape of it—it's just the way Dad peels an orange with his pocket knife. That's it!" He picked it up and dangled it in front of my face. "It's a strip of peel from a round fruit, I bet. See? Some of the fruit is still stuck to the inside."

I groaned. "Why do they keep sending us this *garbage*? What are they doing? What's it supposed to mean?"

"It's gotta mean something," Barry said, dropping it on the table. "We just have to figure it out, that's all. And we *will* figure it out, before anybody else comes butting in."

"Let's see if we can identify any insects," I said.

"I'm going to get Lucy—she knows about that kind of stuff."

"But we have this book," I whined.

"You can stay here and wait, or you can come with me," he said, at the door.

I didn't have any choice. Outside the pine trees, he put two fingers in his mouth and whistled.

"That's *our* whistle," I said. We had used it as a kind of secret signal, back in the old days. "What makes you think Lucy will pay any attention to it?"

"Because I told her to," he said, looking away from me toward the river. It was already dark under the trees. I tried not to wonder if there might be an alien hiding there. "I told her if anything happened, that's how I'd let her know."

"But that whistle's supposed to be a secret, just between us," I said. It was childish, but I couldn't help feeling betrayed. It was just as if he had slapped me.

"We're not eight years old anymore, Harry," he said. "And I can tell Lucy anything I want."

"But why didn't you give her a different—"

"Shhh!" He held up his hand. "Listen."

There was an answering whistle from across the river, faint but jaunty. Lucy did it a lot better than I ever had. My first impulse was to run back to the house by myself and sulk, to make them feel guilty. The trouble was, they wouldn't feel guilty. And I was too curious about the insects to leave.

"Well, this here's a cicada," Lucy said, pointing at a pale brown insect shell on the playhouse floor. "They're everywhere."

"What's a cicada?" Barry asked her.

She stared at him in disbelief. "What's a cicada?" she repeated. "Are you trying to say you don't know what's a cicada?"

"Yeah." He was smiling a little.

She pointed at the door. "A cicada *only* happens to be what makes all that racket out there." She screwed her face up. "You really never heard of a cicada? You don't have 'em in Boston?"

"Guess not," Barry said.

She sighed and rolled her eyes as though the absence of cicadas in Boston was an unforgivable oversight on Barry's part.

"What about these?" Barry said, pointing at a couple of the black bodies. "You see those anyplace but in here?"

She bent over them. "Looks kinda like a beetle. But I couldn't *swear* I'd seen the same one anywhere else."

I checked the book. There were plenty of beetles; none had exactly the same shape or coloring as the playhouse specimens, but some were very similar.

"So maybe they could be coming through, but maybe not," Barry said. He got down on his knees to examine a spiderweb under the sink. "Come over here and look at this spider, Lucy."

Obviously my opinion meant nothing to him. But I went and took a look at it anyway, hoping I would notice something they didn't. It was the same story as the beetles. The spider was tiny and gray and ordinary looking, and could, perhaps, have been one of the species in the book. It was difficult to tell for sure.

"So we still don't know if anything can come through alive," I said.

"But is there any scientific reason why it couldn't?" Barry asked me, running water into the sink.

"There's no proof, one way or the other." I watched the water begin to glow. "I just wish I knew why they're sending all this garbage over here."

"It's like stuff you'd throw away," Lucy said. "Like you'd find in a vacuum cleaner bag."

"Huh?" I turned and stared at her, amazed, as my entire picture of the situation took a sudden twist. "But that's right!" I said. "That's exactly what it's like."

She snorted. "I was only kidding," she said as though I were too dumb to get the joke.

"No, but that's just what it's like." She had never heard of a singularity before, and yet she had come up with a brilliant analogy for its properties. I couldn't help being impressed. "A singularity *is* a giant vacuum cleaner. It sucks up everything that gets close enough to it, whether it's light or dust or . . . or animal hairs."

They exchanged a mystified glance. "*Now* what are you raving about?" Barry said.

"Maybe nobody's over there *deciding* what to send through," I said, the words tumbling out. "Maybe it's accidental, just whatever happens to get near the singularity. It's a huge mindless vacuum cleaner, sucking up debris and sending it over to us. And sometimes it's something valuable, like an animal or an artifact. But mostly it's just trash!"

"I think this time he's really cracked," Barry said insultingly. "It sounds like he's trying to tell us this precious singularity of his is lying around in a town dump somewhere."

"But it *is*!" I shouted. The pattern was finally beginning to make sense. "Look at the kind of stuff that's coming through. It's exactly what you *would* find in a town dump!"

"Rats. That's what you find in a town dump," Lucy said, wrinkling her nose. She wasn't joking now.

"Maybe that's what some of those skeletons were," Barry said. "Alien rats. And maybe there's more coming through."

"Then let me outta here!" Lucy said, with a shiver. but she didn't move from the sink.

Barry flipped off the faucets, and we stared down as the image cleared. It was unfortunate that the subject of rats was on our minds.

Teeth—lots of teeth—were the most prominent feature of the thing now suspended in the event horizon.

14

For a very long time—perhaps even an entire one-hundredth of a second in the outside world—no one spoke.

It was not simply the rows of teeth that made this reflection so stunningly repellent. It was the ferocity of the yawning, scissorlike maw—even frozen in time, this thing hungered to take a bite out of something. It hung below us, the mouth opened so wide that we could see nothing of the rest of it.

The other objects we had previewed, though somewhat elongated, had proved on arrival to be just about the same size as their reflections. But they had appeared close to the surface when we had seen them. This thing was deeper, but was already bigger than any of the other objects. By the time it reached the surface, it looked as though it would be very large indeed.

"Maybe it's distorted," Barry said at last, without conviction. "Maybe we just think it looks like a creature, but it's really something else."

It was a nice try, but it wasn't going to work. Even

if it were a machine and not an animal, it was clearly designed to devour with prodigious efficiency. That's what mouths are for.

"Maybe it just looks nasty to us," Barry tried again. "But everything could be different in another universe. Maybe this is what cute and cuddly looks like over there."

We could see a little bit around the edge of the mouth, where the dark skin curled back around the fangs, caught in the middle of a snarl.

"And maybe it isn't as big as it looks," Barry went on. "Maybe it's really no bigger than a good-sized rat."

"It's far away, Barry," I pointed out. "It looks like it'll be bigger than we are."

"Maybe just the mouth is big, but the rest of it is little," Barry babbled on. "Maybe it's something the size of a mouse with a crocodile-sized head."

We looked at him.

He shrugged. "Well, it was an idea." Violently, he slammed his fist onto the drain knob. The ravenous mouth swirled away down the pipe.

"I think . . . I have to go home now," Lucy said.

He grabbed her by the elbow. "You better not tell anybody."

"Barry," I said. "This monster is going to come through, and you don't want to get people out here to protect us?"

"We don't know it's a monster. We just have—what do they call it?—circumstantial evidence. And we don't even know if it's going to be alive."

"Well, *I'm* not planning to sit here and wait for it in order to find out," I said, backing toward the door.

"That's your decision," Barry said coolly. "But you have no right to prevent me from staying if I want to."

He was still holding on to Lucy's arm. She stood there limply, her lips pressed tightly together.

"But Barry... It's just..." I struggled to find the words. "Even if I *would* let you stay here, and not call the cops, and let you risk your life—which I wouldn't do—it still isn't just your life. If that thing got out, other people might get hurt. You can't do that!"

"Who's going to stop me?"

"*I* will, and Lucy will. Well, Lucy?"

"I don't know what to do." She was clearly reluctant to side with me, the out-of-it, cowardly one. But she was also scared.

"Look, Harry," he said. "We know other animals came through—we saw their skeletons. And nobody got hurt. So why spoil everything just because another one is coming through? I think it's exciting."

"Who says nobody got hurt? *You're* the one who said an alien could have already come through and killed Uncle Ambrose. It could still be around. And you want to let another one out, a big one? This thing could bite your head right off."

"Well it looks far enough away so it won't come through for a couple of days," he said. "Why do anything right away?"

"Sorry. I'm going to call the cops. We've probably

already watied too long." I turned and marched for the door.

"Harry."

His voice was quiet, but harsh. I stopped.

"Harry, if you tell *anybody*—I promise you, I will lock myself in here. And by the time you find anybody to break down the door and drag me out—*if* you can convince anybody to do it—I will be older than you. Old enough so that we won't be twins anymore."

I couldn't say anything. How stupid I had been to imagine he wouldn't have thought of it immediately.

"Come on, Lucy. Let's go down to the river and have a little talk. Harry needs to be by himself and think."

We left the playhouse together. I didn't even turn to watch them walk away, but went straight back to the house. I knew Barry meant what he said. I couldn't think of any way to stop him. It would have been different if I could have gotten my hands on the playhouse keys and thrown them away for good. But since my fiasco down at the river yesterday, Barry was careful to keep the keys with him at all times, even in bed at night. I felt totally helpless.

There was nothing to do but wait—and watch the creature grow.

15

And it did grow as it approached; it grew alarmingly.

One of the most horrifying things about it was that the mouth continued to hide the rest of it. Whether this was due to the angle of its approach or simply the size of the mouth itself, the result was the same—all you could see of it was its mouth. Watching it swim toward you was like staring down the gullet of a moray eel as it prepared to implant its fangs into your face.

As for Barry's threat, I knew it was real. Uncle Ambrose, for whatever reasons of his own, had set the playhouse up very conveniently, with the survival biscuits and the bed and the plumbing facilities. And playhouse time went so fast that Barry wouldn't have to absent himself from real time for very long at all in order to make a big change in his age.

I had calculated that one second outside the playhouse was an hour inside it. That meant that in just about two and a half hours, real time, he'd age a year inside. He could sneak out there in the middle of the night, and I'd never know he was gone until the next morning. And then he'd be my older brother.

And so from that point on, I never lost track of where Barry was. When he was off swimming or exploring with Lucy, I kept watch on the playhouse entrance to make sure he couldn't go in without me. There was no need to be subtle or secretive about it. Everything was out in the open now.

I was pretty sure he wouldn't do it as long as I didn't call the cops, or tell anyone else about the creature. He wanted to escape from me, but it was also clear to both of us that his threat had to be a last resort. Barry suddenly aging a year would create lots of complications—especially with Mom and Dad—that would be better avoided. We were in the middle of our adolescent growth spurt, and a year would make a tremendous difference in his appearance.

But it was still an effective tool for keeping my mouth shut. I knew he *would* do it if I let any information out. And I hated the very idea of it. I couldn't imagine what it would feel like not to be a twin, and I didn't want to find out. He was often mean to me, but even so, I wasn't ready to face the world without him as my twin. And I couldn't stomach the thought of him being my *older* brother.

But how could I just sit around doing nothing while this monster oozed inexorably toward the gate? Maybe it would die on its way through, or be destroyed by the atmosphere. But what if it didn't? Whatever happened then would be our fault. One creature, ravening and destroying, would be bad enough. But what if it wasn't just one creature? What if there was a whole army of invaders? The human race could be destroyed; the earth, taken over by aliens. Perhaps invasion was the real purpose of the singularity. Was I being hysterical or rational? The idea of an invasion wasn't any crazier than all the rest.

But what if I warned people and then it did turn out to be harmless? I'd lose my twin and end up with a hostile older brother who would hate me more than my twin ever had. Barry had me trapped in my own event horizon. I could do nothing. Both alternatives were intolerable.

Over the next couple of days, Barry remained as brash and confident as ever—while I was a nervous wreck, worrying myself sick over the situation.

As always, he was getting his own way. I began to be obsessed with how much he had pushed me around over the last few years. And I had let him do it because giving in was easier than fighting about it. I never cared as much as Barry did about things like sitting in the front seat, so why bother?

But this situation was different. This was something worth fighting about. In a way, it was the worst stalemate of our life, because at least I wasn't *totally* capitulating. I was keeping my distance, hardly talking to him at all. But I wasn't taking any action, either. So it was also the same old pattern again.

Then, on the second night after Barry had made his threat, the pattern changed.

I was brooding in my room, listening to Barry whistle energetically as he got ready for bed. He stopped in my doorway on the way to the bathroom. "Still down in the dumps, Harry?" he said.

I quickly looked away from him.

"Lucy thinks you're strange," he said.

He was just baiting me, so I tried to remain aloof. "I could care less what somebody with an I.Q. of 50 thinks about anything," I said.

"Maybe she's not as stupid as you think," he said, turning to go. "She also said you act more like my little brother than my twin." He sauntered across the hall and pulled the bathroom door shut behind him.

Suddenly I was more furious than I could ever remember being before. I jumped out of bed, growling in my throat like an animal. My first impulse was to dash over to Lucy's house and shake her and scream at her. Instead, I ran wildly into Barry's room, not thinking at all, and threw his pillow off the bed.

The playhouse keys were under the pillow.

The sight of them brought my mind back to work. Barry never would have left them there if he thought I'd take them. He was sure I didn't have the guts to steal anything from his room. And that meant there was a chance he wouldn't check on them before he went to sleep.

I replaced the pillow and started for the stairs with the keys. Then I heard Barry turn off the faucet. He was finished in the bathroom. If I ran for the river now, he'd just take off after me again, like the last time. I hurried to my room, got in bed and turned out the light.

Barry went back to his room. I waited tensely for him to discover that the keys were gone. His light went off. I heard the bedsprings creak as he snuggled down.

126

He hadn't noticed the missing keys. But I wasn't going to make another blunder and run for the river until I was sure he was asleep. Then I could throw them in the deepest pool without any chance of interference.

More like his little brother than his twin. Now she would see. Now they would both see. I'd get rid of the keys, and then Barry would be the helpless one. And I'd be the one in control, the dominant one, the mature one.

Or would I?

What was so mature about throwing the keys in the river? Out of fear, I would be locking up this scientific marvel. And, of course, Barry would make my life miserable. He might even be able to find the keys. And they could still say that throwing them away had been a babyish, cowardly thing to do. *More like his little brother . . .*

But there was one thing I *could* do that would prevent Barry, permanently, from ever pushing me around again.

I sat up slowly in the dark. This new idea could never be called cowardly and certainly not babyish. I didn't like it. The thought of it terrified me. But as I went over the situation in my mind, I saw that it was better than any of the other alternatives. If I had the nerve to do it.

I waited, still seething. I explored every possible consequence. And by the time I was sure Barry had fallen asleep, I had made up my mind.

I got my toothbrush and razor from the bathroom and carefully packed my suitcase. I crept slowly down the stairs, waiting on each step for any noise from Barry's room. He had had an active day and seemed to be sound asleep. But I stayed quiet and cautious, even downstairs. If he woke up now, it would ruin everything.

The books took the most time. I used a cardboard grocery carton, but the books were so heavy that I couldn't carry many at once, so I had to make a lot of trips. Each trip was more tense than the one before, sneaking through the darkness over the squeaky floorboards, constantly afraid of dropping something or bumping into things. But I knew I would thank myself for the books later, so I didn't stop until the dining-room table was cleared.

On the last trip, I filled the carton with food—nonperishable items like candy bars, cookies and peanut butter. For a long moment I stood at the back door, wondering if I was doing the right thing. Suddenly I felt horribly guilty. But I told myself that it wasn't my fault. Barry had forced me to do this. I thought of him lying up there, asleep in bed, and sent him a silent good-bye. Then I plodded across the dark meadow with the carton of food—frequently looking behind to make sure no alien was following me.

After unloading the carton, I got a large supply of fresh batteries from the crate in back of the playhouse and piled them up under the rafters. The ones that had been stored inside would be quite old by now. Finally I went back outside and took out my calculator. I set it on clock mode and placed it several feet from the threshold, propped against a stone, so that it could be easily seen through the doorway. It was 1:30 A.M.

Then I locked myself inside the playhouse.

16

I'd be in here for a year.

The first thing I did was to get in bed and try to go to sleep, so I wouldn't have to think about what I was doing. But sleep seemed impossible. I kept picturing the monster in the sink behind me. Last time we had checked on it, it had still been far from the surface, and we had figured that the earliest it could come through would be tomorrow. I'd be well out of here before then. Even so, my awareness of it so close behind me was not conducive to sleep.

I also felt guilty. Here I was carrying out this thing, and Barry had only threatened to do it. Maybe he had never really meant it—I certainly wouldn't have expected him to have the patience.

Finally I did sleep. When I woke up, hours later, I immediately unlocked the door. For a second I thought the calculator had broken—it still said 1:30.

It was pitch dark out, but the calculator numbers were luminous. I peered closer. What it actually said was 1:30:05. Five seconds had gone by. Or maybe even less, since I hadn't noticed what the seconds said when I had gone in. I would have to start noticing them now.

I let the door slam shut and grabbed a book from one of the piles that covered the floor. I needed to distract myself from the thought of how long I would have to stay in this tiny prison to accomplish anything. It was something called *The Diary and Letters of Madame D'Arblay,* and I opened it at a page describing a glittering ball in a palace full of ladies and officers planning intrigues. I realized that I would not see another human being for a year. I threw the book to the floor.

"You never liked parties anyway, you dope!" I said aloud. But the sound of my own voice made me feel even worse. I gulped down a candy bar, ignoring the thought that now there were only seven left.

I clawed through the trap door and grabbed a package of survival biscuits. I was almost afraid to try one. Barry had grown sick of them after one night. I would have to live on them for a year. On the wrapper, it said that they provided the Recommended Daily Allowance of protein and all other necessary nutrients. I tore open the wrapper and bit into it. It was chewy and tough and bland, with a rancid aftertaste. It made me think of a dish of oatmeal that has been sitting out in the sun for days. It felt dry and crusty and gluey between my teeth.

I fumbled open the jar of peanut butter and scooped up a huge wad of it with my fingers, to kill the taste of the biscuit. It was a big jar—the size we usually went through in a couple of weeks.

"Don't think about it, don't think about it, don't

think about it!" I ordered myself. My voice sounded like a crazy person's. I sobbed and threw myself down on the bed, kicking and beating it with my fists. Then I squeezed the sheet between my fingers and curled up my legs. The sheet was already unpleasantly grimy. It would get a lot grimier.

The day dragged on forever. The place was a disorganized, uncomfortable mess, with books piled all over the floor, and it got messier as I searched through the piles for something interesting to read. But I couldn't concentrate on anything. Every time I managed to read a page, I would start wondering how much time had gone by. I looked outside at the calculator when I was hungry for lunch, but it was only 1:30:07. Every time I looked out into the horrible black night, the clock seemed to be going slower.

I craved another candy bar. But if I ate one now, there would be only six left to last me a year. I knew I'd feel horribly guilty if I gave in. But I was afraid I'd throw up if I ate another one of those disgusting survival biscuits. I banged my fist on the table and sobbed again.

The first milestone came two miserable days later, when the clock in the night outside had finally changed to 1:31. "Congratulations, it's 1:31," I said. "A whole minute. You can do it."

"No! I can't stand it!" I screamed back at myself, pacing, kicking at the tumbled-down mountains of books. There was no floor space left, but I felt too miserable and disorganized to neaten the place up. "What difference does it make?" I asked myself. "Why bother?"

I worried about the creature; I felt guilty about Barry. But I also spent hours brooding about all the horrible things he had done and said to me. It made me furious. I'd never felt this angry in my life. "You're a nasty, mean creep, Barry. I hate you!" I would scream. "And now I'm going to be a whole year older than you. You'll never push me around again!"

"But you're the stupid one, Harry!" I screamed back. "You're the one who ended up in here. You're torturing yourself more than Barry ever did. You're crazy!" I kicked a pile of books across the room and then howled. I had forgotten I was barefoot.

Did I really have to stay here for an entire year? After all, I'd be older than Barry in a couple of weeks or months. But I quickly saw the flaw in that excuse. I couldn't, in the natural world, be Barry's *real* older brother unless I was at least nine months older than he was. Otherwise, I'd just be a kind of freakish anomaly. And I didn't want that. I wanted to be like any ordinary older brother. For that, nine months was necessary. And I might as well make it a year, just to even things off.

To bolster my confidence, I reminded myself that I wasn't *only* doing it to get back at him,—though I knew that was a big part of it. This was also the best way to deal with the creature. I had worked it all out, back in my bedroom. As big brother Harry, I could take control and not have to throw away the keys. I could warn people and at the same time, *show* them exactly what I was warning them about. The old Harry couldn't do that. But big brother

Harry would have the dominance and strength of an extra year. That was why I had to stay.

"So what?" I screamed. "Who cares about warning people?" I threw a shoe at the sink.

As the days went by I began to be aware of an unfamiliar physical restlessness. Unlike Barry, I had always been lethargic, perfectly happy to lie around forever without moving a muscle. But I had never had the chance to do that until now. And now I was beginning to find out that perfect physical inactivity was not so richly satisfying. I stretched and paced obsessively, slipping on books, hardly aware of what I was doing. In my dreams I always seemed to be on the move either chasing Barry or being chased by the monster. In my waking hours I daydreamed about going for a walk and then actually began to hunger for the sensation of running—an activity I had previously detested.

It occurred to me, during the second wretched week, that maybe I could go outside and walk around a bit every once in a while. I reached for my calculator to figure it out—and then remembered I couldn't use it for a year. I screamed and tore the cover off a book and hurled it against the wall. Then I found a pencil and sat down to calculate on the book's title page. It was called *Extraordinary Popular Delusions and the Madness of Crowds*.

My calculations were profoundly disheartening. If I went outside for only five minutes every playhouse day, then it would be morning out there in a mere nine weeks—and I had to age a minimum of nine months. It was hardly worth going outside for less than five minutes, so I would have to do it less often. If I went outside for five minutes once a month, it wouldn't slow my aging down too much—but it would probably be more frustrating than it was worth. But if I went outside for fifteen minutes once a month, then it would take me until almost 7:00, Barry's time, to age a full year—and he might be awake before then. I couldn't take that risk.

How about fifteen minutes once every three months? At that schedule, I would be a year older at 4:41, Barry's time, and I had never known him to wake up that early. And fifteen minutes every three months would give me something to look forward to and be a way of breaking up the year. It would be a kind of holiday.

The first three months would be up when the clock outside said 2:06:30. It was now 1:35:09.

"You lucky thing!" I told myself in a sarcastic falsetto. "In three months you can go outside in the dark for fifteen minutes. Isn't that thrilling? Now you have something wonderful to look forward to."

I jumped up from the table and threw the chair to the floor. But it didn't help. The utter bleakness of my situation struck me then with full force. My itch to move became intolerable, a kind of madness. If I didn't do something drastic, my muscles would take control and drag me screaming out the door. Without thinking I bulldozed the piles of books aside to make a clear space on the floor, threw myself down and began violently doing push-ups, then sit-ups. Only utter desperation could have driven me to such bizarre behavior. But after eight push-ups and ten

135

sit-ups, as I lay there dizzy and gasping, I was aware of a sense of relief in my weakly fibrillating muscles. Calisthenics, detestable as they are, might help my body accept confinement. And they would be a way of marking the endless days. It occurred to me then, for the first time, that establishing a daily routine might be a way to keep from going insane.

And it was a kind of miraculous coincidence that as I lay there on the floor, my pulse taking forever to return to normal, my eyes fell on a spiral notebook at the bottom of one of the piles of books. I must have taken it by accident back in the dark house, but now I reached for it hungrily. And it was unused—one hundred blank, lined sheets.

I had already found a package of long, unsharpened pencils in a little metal kitchen cabinet beside the table. They could be sharpened with a knife, and might last long enough if I was careful. One hundred sheets meant two hundred sides. That gave me half a page of paper a day, with room to spare.

1:35:09 was the most important day so far—the first date in my diary and the beginning of my new routine.

It was a terrible struggle at first, a constant battle not to skip days and fall back into total lolling disorganization. Yet when I did stick to even the easiest routine, I felt like a happy baby. The sense of accomplishment made me so proud of myself that it was in itself encouraging, a kind of reward. It took a period of trial and error for me to develop a good schedule. I had to move activities around and put them in the order that was easiest to stick to. It also had to be rigorous in order to be satisfying. But I persevered. From the very beginning, sticking to the routine made me feel so much better that I knew it was the only way to survive. Strangely enough, it made me feel free in a way I had never experienced before.

By 1:40:19, the pattern had become firmly established.

Now, immediately upon waking up every "morning," I would do my push-ups and sit-ups. I knew they were necessary, but I still hated them and wanted to get them over with right away. Next I would give myself a thorough shave. I had considered growing a beard, but decided against it. If I was clean-shaven, whatever distinguished my seventeen-year-old features from Barry's sixteen-year-old ones would be immediately apparent. And it was another way of killing time. Since I had no mirror, I would go over my face with my fingers to make sure I did a complete job. I worked as slowly and carefully as possible—the longer the process took, the better.

Then came another duty to be dispensed with early in the "day"—a check on the reflection in the sink. As I stared down at the rows of malignant fangs, I would think of Barry. It wasn't that I saw Barry as monstrous. I thought of him because it was he and the creature who shared the responsibility for my being here. They were also both trapped in time—statues—while I lived, and moved, and grew. That knowledge gave me a boost of confidence and increased my determination not to give in to either of them.

After that I would put on clean clothes and sit

down to breakfast. I had found a jar of five hundred superstrength multivitamin capsules in the cabinet, and I swallowed one before I ate. As I gnawed on the survival biscuit and washed it down with glasses of cold water, I would concentrate, with all the clarity and attention to detail I could muster, on the breakfast room at home. I thought of my place at the table, the blue woven placemats, the white dishes. I thought of soft-boiled eggs, icy orange juice and hot buttered toast. I thought of the red checked curtains and the flowering plants on the windowsill. But most of all I thought about the sunlight pouring through the window, warm on my face, glittering on the edge of my glass. In the winter months sometimes, the angle and intensity of the light would be so dazzling that I would have to squint against the glare in order to see Barry's face across the table. "Would you like me to pull the shade down, so you can see better, honey?" Mom would say. "No thanks, it feels good," I would tell her. I thought about that a lot.

After breakfast I would clear the table and make the bed. Then I would return to the table with my current "serious" book—I usually had two or three going at once, a lighter one and a heavier one. I would pretend I was studying for a test and would be responsible later for a thorough knowledge of the material. I didn't have enough paper to take notes, but there were plenty of pencils for underlining, and I would fold down the corners of important pages. I would work hard at it, going over and over difficult passages until I was sure I understood them, often reading them aloud.

Lunch would be another unadorned survival biscuit and water. I had calculated that if I ate one-half teaspoon of peanut butter a day, the jar would last for a year. I saved it for supper. During lunch, I would concentrate on the school cafeteria. For the last year or so, since Barry had stopped sitting with me, lunch at school had been rather a frantic experience. It would start with trying to hook up with a friend on the way to the cafeteria, so that we'd be in line together, and then, I hoped, automatically sit together. If I didn't find someone in line, I would take my food quickly and then stand there with my full tray, scanning the room for empty places beside people I knew. Often there weren't any. Then I would have to go through the ordeal of sitting alone, trying not to feel horribly conspicuous.

I would tell myself that it was really much pleasanter here in the playhouse. But I would still try to reconstruct in my head the noisy babble of conversation, the clatter of trays and silverware, the sloppy joes on soft buns, watery canned beans and pink Jell-O cubes quivering under blobs of nondairy topping. I had complained about the food at school, as everyone did. It seemed scrumptious to me now.

After lunch I did my chores. In the first weeks there had been the books to organize, the ones I had brought over as well as the ones that had already been here. I arranged them by general categories and then within the categories, alphabetically by the author. I set them spine outward along the walls, and under the bed and table and sink, piled up on top of each other in horizontal rows, since there were no shelves. Once I had the books organized, I would use the chore time for sweeping and dusting. The insects and the silvery powder continued to accumulate on the floor under the sink, though not as rapidly, of course, as it had seemed to happen from outside the playhouse. Another chore I did at this time was the laundry. There was plenty of hand soap, stored up under the rafters with the survival biscuits, and the sink was nice and large—just as if, once again, Uncle Ambrose had envisioned spending a lot of time in here. The wet clothes could be draped over the rafters—where it was warm, as in an attic—and they would dry there in a couple of days.

When the chores were done I would turn to my lighter reading. By "light," I basically mean fiction, though for the most part it was not at all what I would have considered light reading in the old days. There were novels like *Moby-Dick*, *Anna Karenina* and *The Way of All Flesh*, books that people in school groaned about having to read—and would frequently avoid altogether by obtaining study guides. English had never been my strong point, but now, not surprisingly, I found these books vastly entertaining, often exclaiming or laughing out loud as I read. Before I realized it, I would be at the end of what I would have expected to be an interminable chapter, and I would have to force myself to read more slowly, so as not to use them up too fast. There was a certain satisfaction in the knowledge that I was doing a significant amount of the rest of life's homework.

When I had first organized the library, I discovered with nearly hysterical excitement that Uncle Ambrose had a small collection of paperback mysteries and even some science fiction. With my newly developing willpower, I managed to prevent myself from devouring all of these books immediately. I made a pact with myself that I would read one of these books only after finishing two of the more ponderous works. By spacing them out throughout the year, I would always have some deliciously fast-paced tidbit to look forward to.

I would consider late afternoon to have arrived when I began to be hungry for supper. But supper, the most sumptuous meal of the day, had to be put off for as long as possible. I would close the book, take off my clothes, and proceed to the next step in my routine, jogging in place. This activity had come to be a pleasure—not a penance like calisthenics. Therefore it belonged toward the end of the day. Moving my legs up and down stimulated my brain, and I would relive amusing conversations I had once had with Barry, or with friends, or with Mom and Dad. I would remember movies and trips in great detail. I would go over in my head what I had read that day and try to decide what were the most important facts, the most telling insights about people. I would jog until I was sweating copiously, leaving drops on the floor with every step, and my throat was dry.

Then I would sit down on the metal chair and wait for the sweat to evaporate and let my mind wander. But very often my mind, which had been stimulated by the running, would just go blank. I would think about nothing at all, staring at the wall and feeling the blood coursing through my veins. After a while I began to notice that this meditative rest period left me with an unexpected feeling of well-being. It was terrible in here, yet at this time of day I actually felt happy. I never would have believed it possible.

Then I would take my bath, standing beside the sink. It wasn't necessary to fill it up and create the disturbing reflection—I could get wet all over by sticking the various parts of my body under the tap.

I didn't get dressed again after my bath. In the morning, it was important to put on clean clothes just as a way of making it seem like morning. But once that had been accomplished, I didn't need clothes. I enjoyed spending the evening without anything on. That was something I wouldn't have a chance to do very often when I returned to the real world.

I would fill the glass with water now and sip it slowly, thinking about sitting around before dinner with Mom and Dad at home. It was during this aperitif period that I would allow myself, for the first time all day, to open the door and check on the "date." I had learned very early on that it was vital to my emotional well-being *not* to open the door until my biological clock told me that it was evening. Nothing was more important than to preserve the illusion that day and night were occurring. All day I would keep busy, and at frequent intervals imagine sunlight coming through the windows at home, sunlight filling the meadow outside the playhouse. To open the door at any other time but evening would bring home to me the terminally depressing fact that it was always night out there, and always would be. There was no mere six months of darkness, such as inhabitants of the arctic zone endure. This was an entire year of it. It was necessary to avoid that reality by any means, however artificial.

Checking the clock was inevitably disappointing, but could not be avoided. There was also the terrible temptation, once the door was open, to escape. And so I would always do it after running, when I felt most at peace with myself, and just before dinner, which functioned as my reward for closing the door and staying inside.

For my appetizer, I would have one potato chip. I had a big one-pound bag of them. When I had first devised my menu, I had thought I might have to eat the potato chips quickly, instead of spacing them over the entire year—once opened, the chips would go soggy in about a week. But I actually didn't *want* to eat them all at once. I wanted to have them to look forward to.

And it was the potato-chip dilemma that had given me a brilliant idea: There was no reason why the *chips* had to age a year. So why not keep them outside on the threshold? Outside, they'd only be sitting around for a few hours, not long enough to get stale. The same was true for the peanut butter and the cookies and candy bars and vitamin pills, and even the survival biscuits. I piled the food up outside the door. Animals wouldn't be a problem, since the door would be opened by me every twenty-four seconds, their time, which wouldn't given them a chance to eat much.

And so when I opened the door to check on the time, I would snatch my food for dinner and the next day's breakfast and lunch. It gave me a little charge to be reaching out into real time, like a scientist poking his hands into one of those insulated boxes with padded gloves, working with hazardous materials.

There was no reason why I couldn't keep milk and cereal and bread and butter and fresh fruit out there as well, I now realized. On my three-month walk, I would get these items from the house. They would make life a lot pleasanter in here. For now, however, my dinner consisted of two survival biscuits sandwiched together with a succulent half teaspoon of peanut butter.

After dinner I listened to music. I had brought my portable tape player and four cassettes. I had already been quite familiar with all four tapes, and would soon grow to know them so well that I hardly even heard them as music. What was important about listening to them was that they were sounds coming from outside myself; a real, physical reminder that the world did exist out there; a promise that someday I would return to the world.

Next I would write in my diary, dating each entry with the time on the clock. The entries were not particularly gossipy or suspenseful. But it gave me a chance to note what I had been reading and what I was thinking and daydreaming about. And it helped tremendously, especially when I was depressed—which was often, at the beginning—to express my emotions. Though the diary could never respond, writing in it did have the quality of speaking to another person. That made it one of the most important activities of all.

I was now looking forward to my first fifteen-minute walk at the end of three months as if it were Christmas. I had made other plans to go along with it. What if I didn't eat my second candy bar until the day of my walk? Then I could eat two candy bars that day without ever going over my quota of one every month and a half. I had decided to save other things up as well and make it into a real holiday celebration.

I was reminded of the religious practice—which we had never observed in family—of fasting before an important holiday feast. If I didn't eat any peanut butter at all for twelve days before The Great Walk, then I would be able to gorge on two whole table-spoons at one sitting. According to the label, there were twenty-four chocolate chip cookies in the un-opened bag on the threshold. I vowed I would eat cookies only on Great Walk days. That would allow me to overindulge on eight of them on each holiday.

There would, of course, be only three holidays during my stay in the playhouse, at the three-month, six-month, and nine-month milestones. The final quarter, at the end of twelve months, would for obvious reasons require no special preparations to make it the greatest holiday of all.

It was one evening when I was washing my hair that I noticed how long it was getting, almost cover-ing my ears. My first thought was that I would have to cut it. There was a scissors in the cabinet drawer. It wouldn't be easy without a mirror; it would proba-bly look terribly hacked and uneven. But it was beginning to take quite a while to wash it and even longer for it to dry.

But what did that matter? I had plenty of time to kill; the more time-consuming activities I could make for myself, the better. I had never been allowed to let my hair grow much before, and was a little curious about how long it would get in a year. Would it reach as far as my waist or possibly even farther? This was probably the only chance I'd ever have to find out. It would be an amusing experiment, one more way of marking time.

Immensely long hair would also make me look strikingly unlike Barry and would emphasize all the other differences there would be in our appearances. I decided not to cut it at all.

It was satisfying, as the weeks went by, to see the diary pages fill up. And as the days progressed, they seemed to go faster. Before I knew it, it was 2:00:54, and there were only two weeks left before The Great Walk. Two days after that, on 2:01:42, I had to stop eating peanut butter for supper in order to save up the two tablespoons for the feast. But that was easy. I was so excited about The Great Walk that I didn't have much of an appetite.

And then it was 2:03:42, and there was a week left; then two days; and then I was writing in my diary on the eve of The Great Walk. I didn't expect to sleep much, but somehow I did. I opened my eyes; the wonderful day had arrived.

I had told myself that I didn't need to observe my routine on The Great Walk Holiday. And yet the first thing I did, without even thinking, was my thirty push-ups and fifty sit-ups. Then I carefully shaved, then I checked on the reflection, then I had my usual breakfast. My routine had become second nature to me. I didn't even *want* to break from it.

I went through the entire day as usual, not even eating one of my eight cookies or two candy bars. The feast, of course, would come at the very end of the day, *after* The Great Walk itself. I would need something very powerful to get me back inside the playhouse.

I washed socks and underwear, I jogged in place, I bathed. And then, suddenly, I was standing at the open door with the flashlight and the keys. The calculator said 2:06:38. The moment had arrived.

My emotions were so powerful I was almost in pain. I stood without moving, inside the door. Then I said, "Happy Holiday, Harry."

For the first time in three months, I stepped outside.

17

It was not like the time I had run out and found myself for a few seconds in a frozen world. This time, I let the seconds elapse as I slowly crossed the threshold to minimize the shock of transition on my body. And so I stepped out into a world that was already alive.

But it was still a shock. Too many things happened at once. I clamped my hands over my ears, nearly deafened by the roar of the faint breeze, the thundering of the shallow little river, the wild shrieking of the drowsy insects. The reek of freshly mown grass hit me. The warm living air brushed across my bare skin. My knees gave way and I toppled forward. I could feel each individual blade of grass and the stored heat of the sun in the earth.

I rolled over. My face was a foot away from the calculator. It was racing madly, dementedly. It was already past 2:08, and the hours—which had suddenly become seconds—were disappearing so fast I could hardly see them. I had only until 2:21. I scrambled to my feet.

I set the flashlight down on the threshold; I could see well enough without it. I still had the keys in my left hand. With my right hand, I picked up the calculator. Then I ran past the sundial, out of the circle of pines and into the very center of the meadow.

It was a clear night. The millions of stars trembled and were blurred by tears as it dawned on me that they were *not* painted on a seven-foot-high ceiling. They were infinitely far away, and there was nothing between them and me. I reached toward them, feeling as though my body were growing like a magic beanstalk, stretching to fill the vast emptiness. I was swaying, turning, drunk with the sensation of endless space.

A small dark shape whizzed past my head. I shrieked, and then laughed. "Hi, bat!" I cried. It was the first living creature I had encountered in a long time, and I loved it for its reckless speed and agility. From somewhere nearby came the spooky inquisitive cry of an owl. It was talking to me! "Hi, owl!" I answered. "Happy hunting!"

Then I pressed my hand to my mouth and giggled. The angular silhouette of the house was only twenty yards away. I'd better be careful or I'd wake up Barry. I turned back to the sky. The moon, which was full, drenching the meadow in silver, hung just above a distant line of trees. I couldn't tell which way it was going, but I hoped that it was rising and not setting, so that it would still be around on my next two holidays.

That reminded me of the time. With a sick pang in my stomach, I looked at the hateful calculator—the clock that was always my enemy, moving too slowly when I was in the playhouse and too quickly out here. It flashed frantically, now past 2:15. I had barely six minutes left.

Then I heard another sound, a sound so compelling in its loneliness and melancholy that again my shaky legs gave way. I cried for real now, on my knees in the meadow, listening to the long-drawn-out wail of the train. To hear that sound in the middle of the night had always meant isolation, as though I and the distant, disappearing engineer were the only two human beings awake in the world. Now I pictured the sleeping passengers curled against each other in the dim coaches, the porters playing cards in the club car, a baby crying, all rushing away from me through some far-off cornfield. The sense of isolation was multiplied, a crushing weight that pinned me to the earth. And yet, at the same time, it was the most achingly beautiful sound I had ever heard.

"No! You *can't* ruin my holiday!" I shouted at the train, and jumped to my feet. The calculator still gave me five minutes. I took off. This was my chance to move through space, to run. I mustn't waste one more precious second of it.

Suddenly I knew what I wanted to do, though five minutes wasn't much time for it. I paused to drop the keys and the calculator under the sundial, and then headed toward the river, upstream to the left, where the pool was. The pool that had seemed uninviting to me on that sunny day so long ago was now, in the fleeting vertiginous moonlight, irresistible.

Through the darkness under the trees, relishing

the underbrush scratching me, the sharp stones beneath my feet. The lively, noisy river was another living thing, and I hurried toward it. I splashed through the shallow water toward the smooth pool with its pale reflected cliff, a ghostly shape. The bottom dropped away. I lunged forward and as my body went under, I kicked hard with my legs, diving for the bottom.

Swimming at night had always terrified me. I would imagine the dark water aswarm with invisible monsters and emerge in a panic before my hair was wet. But I was too busy now to invent any monsters. To be immersed in the tingling water was an enchantment; to stretch my arms against it, supported and buoyed by this magical substance, was like flying in a dream. My head broke the surface. I hung beneath trembling leaves, dappled by moonlight, weightless as I treaded water. And I could feel the tug of the current like a friend pulling me by the hand, urging me to follow.

My time was up. And miraculous as it was to be out here, I was not tempted to stay. Unless I went back into the playhouse at once, the last three months would all have been for nothing. I was committed now.

But it wasn't easy. I struggled up the bank and ran for the sundial, shivering a little. And I asked myself, If the real world is this wonderful after only three months, what will it be like after a year? I still had that to look forward to.

I set the calculator up outside the door. It read

2:21:41; I was three seconds late. I scooped up my allotted candy bars and cookies and dashed inside.

And there I was again, under the glaring light bulb in the bleak, stuffy little room. It seemed smaller than ever now; the walls had shrunk. Bugs and cobwebs were everywhere. Whenever I moved, I bumped into something. And I had forgotten how rank and stale the air was, like the air in a subway toilet.

I would never be able to stay in here for three more months—or even a week. I must have dreamed I'd been here that long. I'd go crazy.

Then I realized that in my excitement at being outside, I had forgotten to bring any fresh food from the house—the milk and apples and orange juice and bread and butter and cereal I had been looking forward to. Now I'd have to wait another three months. To compensate, I gobbled down my full quota of two candy bars and eight cookies. They were the first sweets I'd eaten in three months, and they tasted cloying and greasy. I vomited them up two minutes later.

But my body's rejection of its reward was not the worst part of my return to the playhouse. That came the next morning. Numbly, I began my routine, doing my best not to think about how many days were left before the next holiday. I let the sink fill up, then turned off the tap and peered gloomily into the reflection.

The mouth had jumped suddenly closer.

18

I was terrified. It was moving faster now. The jaws filled half the sink. I had to get out of here and run for help.

I gripped the edge of the sink and closed my eyes. And I realized then that there had been no change in its rate of approach. In the fifteen minutes that I had been outside last night, over five weeks had gone by inside the playhouse. Naturally the monster would move a lot closer in five weeks than it did in one day. I should have expected this to happen, but somehow I hadn't thought of it. In any case, it would still be a while before the monster came through.

I emptied the sink and pulled on my clean clothes. Since I had eaten no peanut butter last night after being sick, I allowed myself an entire tablespoon on my breakfast survival biscuit. I needed something to help me get over the shock I had just been through.

The first day was terrible. But as more days went by, I began to cheer up. There was something comforting about my routine. I was proud of myself for sticking to it for so long, but I also realized that the three months I had spent in here had not been so very awful. Maybe I *could* make it through another quarter until the next holiday. And then my stay would be half over.

And I'd make sure that the next holiday was better. I could do more than just save up childish goodies for a feast. I could plan my activities carefully, so that not one priceless nanosecond would be wasted.

A nanosecond, I had recently learned from a physics book, was one billionth of a second. Just to kill time, I got out my pencil to figure out how much time went by in here for every nanosecond in the outside world. Not much, it turned out—only about four millionths of a second. In fact, the difference did not become significant until I got all the way up to the millisecond—one thousandth of a second—range. One millisecond in real time was over three and a half whole seconds in here.

I stopped referring to my holiday as The Great Walk because I knew now that fifteen minutes wasn't enough time for much of a walk at all. Instead, I began calling it Saturnalia, after the ancient Roman festival. The name had the ring of wild revelry to it, the perfect contrast to the scholarly, ascetic life I lived in here.

Calisthenics, shaving, monster check, breakfast, serious reading, lunch, chores, light reading, jogging, meditation, bath, aperitif, time check, dinner, music, diary, bed. It was a good schedule, full enough so that no single activity lasted for too long, varied enough so that each activity was a refreshing change from the one before. I wasn't nearly as bored as I had expected to be. My sense of purpose grew. And it continued to be immensely gratifying to see the diary pages fill up:

2:25:18
My hair is an inch below my ears now. I've been wearing it tied back in a rubber band, but tonight I tried braiding it after it dried. It didn't work. But I'll keep trying. I bet I'll be an expert at it before long. I also thought it might be a little darker than before, but it's hard to tell because I have nothing to compare it to. So I cut off a few strands from the front. Now I can check it every once in a while to see if the color is changing. That gave me the idea that every month or so I should measure the amount of beard hairs in my razor from one shave, to see if my beard is getting thicker—and save them too, to see if it's getting darker.

2:25:42
Didn't have the space to finish last night. Then I got the idea to measure my growth by marking a line on the wall, so I did it. Why didn't you think of that at the beginning, you dumb jerk? Today I was reading in *The Golden Bough* about how during the week of Saturnalia, the Roman slaves were allowed to do anything they wanted—they could shout at their masters and even trade places with them, ordering them to wait on them. I tried to figure out how I could imitate that during my own Saturnalia. But who is the slave and master in here? I thought maybe I was the slave to my schedule and could break it on that day, but I didn't want to before. And anyway, the schedule is good, it's what saves me. Then I thought, I am the slave of Time. But can't see how to turn the tables on Time.

2:26:06

After I wrote that last night, I realized that I already *have* turned the tables on Time. That's what I'm doing in here. I decided how much and how fast I wanted to age, and I'm controlling it by figuring out how much time to spend inside and how much time outside. But when I go out there on Saturnalia, then Time will be the master again, our positions reversed. He'll make that fifteen minutes go by so fast. And I won't be able to do anything about it. Or will I? Maybe, if I plan it right. That's why it's so important to plan it. If I'm smart enough, maybe I can make that fifteen minutes a lot longer.

2:34:25

It's over a month already since the first holiday (hooray!), but it doesn't seem that long. Amazing. Last night I dreamed I was in Miss Stevens' English class. We were having a test, and I hadn't done any of the reading (why would I dream *that*?) and didn't know any of the answers. Then Miss Stevens came over and kneeled down by my desk and hugged me and whispered, "Your mother told me and it's all right. Just don't tell anybody else." But Barry was sitting next to me, and he knew what she had said and he was mad. I ran after him, but the hallway was so crowded with kids, and he was faster than me. Then they were all screaming at me, "You'll never catch him!" Then I woke up, and when I saw where I was, I actually felt *relieved*. Because now it's Barry who will never catch up with me.

2:42:31

Tonight when I was meditating after jogging, I imagined what it would be like to be floating around

outside, looking at the world. I was still on playhouse
time, so it was a frozen world. It was such a calm
feeling, looking at the motionless leaves and rabbits,
the motionless bat hanging over the meadow. I had all
the time I could ever want, so it didn't matter if I
made a mistake now and then or if things didn't go
right that day. Then I floated over to the river. I
looked at a stationary rock sticking up out of the water
in the fastest part of the rapids. By staring hard at the
edge of the rock, I could just barely see the foam
creeping past it. It didn't *flow* exactly, but it very
gradually undulated. It was like a river of barely
oozing plastic. If I didn't have the rock to compare it
to, I wouldn't have been able to see it move at all.

2:42:55
Today when I was looking at the creature, I almost
forgot, for a minute, how scary it was. Maybe it's
because I'm taking control. As soon as I get out of
here—less than a couple of hours in real time—I'll
warn people about it, I'll show them what it is. Barry
won't be able to stop me. It's too late to stop me now.
Maybe that's why the creature doesn't seem so threatening to me. . . . And why I don't hate it so much in
here anymore.

My situation wasn't as bad as being stranded on a
desert island, not knowing whether I would ever be
rescued. I knew I'd be out in less than a year. And it
was a lot better than being a prisoner of war or even
a jailed convict. There was no torture in here, no
hostile guards or violent inmates. There was no hard
labor, nothing imposed on me at all. I wasn't here
against my will and that made a tremendous difference. I had chosen it. I had stopped blaming Barry

for what was happening. I didn't want to relinquish the responsibility to him. I wanted it myself.

And in what seemed like less time than it had taken for the first quarter to go by, it was 2:57:56, the eve of Saturnalia. I noted in my diary that tomorrow I would be six months older. I did not break from my routine on the holiday, for the most part. I was more entrenched in it than ever now. I even wondered vaguely if I might miss the routine when I went back to the real world.

But I didn't jog in place on the holiday for a very specific reason, and I didn't bathe. When it was time to meditate, I turned out the light and sat in the darkness. I waited for about half an hour, which was the length of time I usually seemed to meditate. By then, I felt in control of myself, and very open, ready to absorb as much as possible. And my pupils were fully dilated now, in the almost complete darkness of the playhouse.

When I opened the door, it was silvery bright out there. The calculator said 2:58:20. Breathing evenly, I bent forward, the keys in my left hand. Then I bounded from the threshold, scooped up the calculator without a break in my stride, and was off and running.

I knew, from my daily jogging in place, that a fifteen-minute run would be effortless for me now—I wouldn't even be out of breath at the end of it. But I'd be able to cover so much more ground than before, soak up so many experiences that last time I had missed. I was already out of the circle of pines and into the meadow before the cascade of sounds whooshed through my ears and I felt the wind move. The last digit on the calculator languidly dissolved and became a one. Only one second had gone by, and I was already well on my way.

I had decided against taking time to get fresh food from the house. My diet, as it was, seemed perfectly adequate—I felt more energetic than ever and hadn't once been sick. Even if my diet hadn't been healthy, a few apples and a quart of milk wouldn't improve it much over a period of six months. What I was eating was dull, but that didn't bother me much anymore. My priorities had changed. The next fifteen minutes were too important to waste on gathering unnecessary food.

I tore across the meadow, through the opening in the vine-covered hedge and out onto the road, my braid bouncing on my neck. I thumped along in my bare feet, kicking up dust. There was a breeze, but the night was hot, and soon the dust was clinging to my damp skin. It felt wonderful.

The little road twisted and turned, tall corn on one side, thick trees on the other. Around a corner I came to a pimpled metal bridge. I leaned over the railing and looked down at the water. I tried to follow individual bubbles as they whirled through the waves and foam, but they went too fast for my eyes to keep track of them. I remembered how the river barely crept along on playhouse time. But I didn't want to think about that now. I sped across the bridge.

The trees suddenly leapt toward me as a patch of yellow light raked across them. The river was so noisy, I hadn't heard the engine, the crunch of tires of gravel. I barely had time now to get out of the middle of the road and no time to hide. The blinding headlight glared directly into my eyes, and I could see nothing but two dazzling spots as the vehicle rumbled past me. It clanged across the bridge and then came to a noisy halt. A door slammed.

I had forgotten to get dressed. Whoever was in the car had seen me, long-haired and naked and on the run. And now they were blocking the way to the playhouse, and soon it would be time for me to start back. I thought of following the river. But I didn't know whether the playhouse was upstream or downstream from here, and the river's course was so winding that it would take far too long even if I didn't get lost. I had to get past the car. And then, somehow, I had to get through Uncle Ambrose's gate without being seen, so that they would not follow me and investigate.

Footsteps approached. "Okay, what's the hurry?" twanged a deep male voice.

The glare had faded from my eyes now, and I saw that I was really in trouble. Against the moonlit sky I could see a long antenna sticking up from the back of the car, and the cylindrical shape of a light fixture in the middle of the roof. The tall figure confronting me had something on his head that looked a lot like a visored cap.

A flashlight beam stung my eyes. "Awright, kid. Who are you and what you doin' out here?"

Would the cop believe me if I told him who I was and why I was in Sushan, and if I said that I couldn't sleep and was just going for a moonlight walk? Probably not, under the circumstances. How would he know the house wasn't still vacant and that I wasn't a vandal? I would have to prove my story by taking him back to the house and showing him keys and documents. It would takes months and months of playhouse time and wake up Barry for sure. Everything would be ruined.

But how could I just run away without any explanation? If I tried to get back to the house, he'd catch up with me and see where I was going and check the place out. If I ran in the other direction and then hid in the woods, he might not find me—but he would probably go back and check on the house later. It would look as though I were running away from the house for some suspicious reason.

"Say somethin', kid. Where you runnin' to? What you doin' with that gizmo?"

"Timing myself," I said. It was the first thing I'd said to anyone else in six months. But it didn't feel strange to be speaking out loud, because I had been talking to myself a lot. "I'm a runner," I said. "Just practicing, trying to improve my time."

"At this time a night? In the nude?"

"I . . . It's the coolest time to run," I said. "And there's nobody on the road to see me, no traffic or anything." I held up my hands. "What *else* would I be doing with just my timer and my keys?"

"I dunno. But it seems mighty peculiar. You live with your family or roommates or you married or what?"

"Married? Oh . . . uh, with my family."

"What's your name and address? I gotta run you home and check—"

We both jumped as a horn behind us blared out "Shave and a haircut, two bits." Tires shrieked, and a convertible full of laughing teenagers zoomed past. It missed the police car by inches and sheered through a row of corn as it careened around the next turn.

"Drunk, I bet," the cop said, running for his car. "Gotta stop 'em before they get killed—or kill somebody else. But I'll be watchin' for you, and if I see you runnin' around like that again, you'll be in trouble." He jumped into his car and took off after them.

It was 3:11. I had two minutes to get back to the playhouse. As I ran, the events of the last few minutes raced around in my head. I had hoped to get much further along the road and to get back in time for a swim. But I wasn't disappointed that my plans had been botched. What had happened had been tense, but exciting—and excitement was exactly what I needed on my holiday.

I was amazed by my luck. I would have been in a mess if those kids hadn't come along. But now the cop didn't know who I was or that I had anything to do with Uncle Ambrose's house. And he wouldn't find me on the road again tomorrow night.

It was 3:13:02 when I went back inside the playhouse. I was ravenous, but after I had eaten my extra ration of peanut butter on three survival biscuits, one candy bar turned out to be enough.

It was not until I wrote the incident in my diary that I saw what I had just done.

Yes, I was in here to grow a year older than Barry for purely personal reasons. But I had also thought that part of my motivation was to take control away from Barry so that I could warn people about the creature.

But I hadn't warned the cop; I hadn't even *thought* of it. All I had wanted to do was get rid of him. It was crazy. I had suddenly forgotten about the creature, just when I had the perfect opportunity to do something about it.

As though something else—not Barry at all—was preventing me from interfering with its progress.

19

The last six months were very different from the first and not just because they went by so much more quickly.

When I checked on the reflection the day after Saturnalia, the mouth had grown so large that the teeth filled the sink. It was already easily big enough to bite off a human head—and it would be bigger still when it came through.

As before, only the mouth and teeth were visible, but the details were a lot more distinct. I could see a kind of crease on either side where the top and bottom jaws met, like the line between the two blades of a scissors. There was a round pimple or nodule where the crease ended. It made me think of a hinge. Inside the mouth, behind the rows of teeth, the throat seemed to be made up of interlocking cylinders as though the head were telescoping toward me.

To distract myself, I checked on my progress. I was nearly an inch taller than I had been when I measured my height three months ago. When I got

out, I might be as much as two inches taller than
Barry. I had already noticed that my clothes were
getting to be much too short, though not too tight.
My hair, unbraided, fell to my shoulders. It seemed
several shades darker than the sample I had saved,
closer to brown than to blond. My beard hairs from
the razor were a good deal darker than that, and one
day's worth filled three-quarters of a teaspoon instead of barely a half.

I couldn't see my face, but my body had changed.
Of course I was thinner. The softness around my
belly was gone, and I could count my ribs. But I
wasn't undernourished. Not only was I taller, but
there were muscles on me that had never been there
before. By now, I was doing fifty push-ups and one
hundred twenty sit-ups, and running for what seemed
like an hour.

For the first few days after my second holiday, I
worried about my peculiar behavior out on the road.
Why hadn't I warned the cop? Was it just because I
wanted to keep growing for the full year? Or had the
creature—or some power from the singularity—
influenced me to forget? I had been living within its
force field now for six months. Had it altered my
brain somehow?

I plunged back into my routine, which was, I
knew, something completely my own. It was like a
home I was constructing with painstaking care; and
every day I worked on it, it became stronger, more
impregnable. I was the third little pig, the smart
one, in his house of bricks. All problems lay in wait,
like the wolf, just outside. The routine would make

them harmless—by providing a foundation, an identity that gave me control. As the days passed, I didn't stop wondering about things that seemed unanswerable. I just worried about them less.

I was jogging in place one evening—the date was 3:20:08, according to my diary—and thinking about an incident in a book I had read. I tried to place it exactly, since it was part of my routine to be specific about my reading. It must have been a mystery, because it was about a very clever crime, a barely avoided auto accident caused by fast-growing corn completely hiding an intersection on a highway. Could the name of the book have been *Ears*?

I was about to giggle. Then I placed the incident and choked. My heart rate would have speeded up if it hadn't already been elevated from running. I stumbled. I started to sit down. No! That would be a mistake! I began running again, harder than ever.

But I still felt shocked, because it hadn't been an incident in a book. It was something that had happened to Barry and me and the lawyer in a nearby cornfield.

Or in another world.

When the full hour was up, and not before, I sat down to meditate. I concentrated on what had just happened. And it wasn't fanciful at all to see the cornfield incident as an event in another world. It really was another world out there. It was the earth, with its fixed time stream. And I wasn't in it anymore.

Part of me wanted to cut off that train of thought immediately. But another part—the part that was supported by the foundation I was building—refused to hide from it. I wasn't part of the earth in here. Nor was I part of the other universe though I was close to it. Then where was I?

I was in between the two universes. I was in the singularity that connected them.

Barry was still back in that other world. I had left him permanently behind. A part of me had been cut away, like an amputated limb. I was isolated as I had never been before. I was totally alone.

No. Not alone.

There was one other entity that shared this fantastic and paradoxical perch with me. My only companion. And I was closer to it than I was to Barry now.

I got up and ran water into the sink.

3:23:19

I don't meditate much these days. Instead, I stand at the sink and watch The Approaching One. It is in one universe; I'm in another. Between and around us lies the time-bending interface where the two universes meet, the awesome singularity. The Approaching One hovers in the eternal instant of the event horizon while I rocket through time. But we are bonded together as if the singularity were a kind of womb that encloses us. Every instant we grow closer. I stare at the shiny cones of Its teeth, each ending in a pinpoint of light. Are they teeth, or are they eyes? Or are they some organ or mechanism unknown to me? Is there a head, is there even a brain behind the mouth? Or is there only a mouth on a telescoping gullet? I study It for signs of sentience, for an indication of life, a flicker of communication.

3:31:27

Today I looked back at the entry from 2:42:31, when I imagined what the world outside looks like from playhouse time. And then I couldn't help thinking what it looks like from the point of view of the event horizon and The Approaching One. To be frozen, while the rest of the universe accelerates:

Bats shoot over the meadow, humming like bullets. The river is a blur, a streak of white fire. The stars roll. The moon plummets into the trees. The sun shoots up and whirls across the sky, ever faster, until night and day blink on and off like a shutter, a flickering old movie, and then become too quick for the eye, an unchanging bluish gray. Leaves vanish from the trees, there is a bright flash of snow, an explosion of green sweeps across the world and is gone again, until the seasons themselves are a permanent pale green mist. Trees break from the earth and grow, branches wriggling skyward like worms. A vast ocean rises and then evaporates in a puff of steam. The sun swells and hungrily devours the black cinder of the earth. And through all the violent activity, The Approaching One in the event horizon remains calm and unchanged.

3:40:01
For days at a time I forget entirely about that other world. I read about it; but I'm reading about a fantasy world. When I do remember that I had a life there, I'm startled. It seems so frantic and busy, flooded with pain. It's a relief to be in here now. The feeling is like . . . long ago, when I would wake up from a nightmare, and it would slowly dawn on me that the terror had only been a dream, and everything was all right in reality. That's how I feel when I think of that other world.

I didn't go out on the third holiday. It wasn't because I lost track of time. On 3:49:30, I just didn't feel like going out. It seemed as though it would be an interruption. But I was aware that not going out would change my growth schedule, so that I would now be a year older on 4:26:00.

3:53:13

It seems absurd to me now that I skipped my third holiday. Why did I do that? And my diary entries from that period sound a little absurd as well. So philosophical! As though they were written by someone else. Maybe I was going through some sort of phase, a growth stage. But not one of those awful sounding ones, like "oral" or "anal," that psychiatrists write about as though they were describing the multiplication tables. It was my own phase, unique to me. And I'm coming out of it now. Maybe it *was* a brain wave, or force field, from The Approaching One. Maybe It did something to me, changed me. Should I be scared? I'm not. It happened. Why bother worrying about something that you can't change? I know, people told me that for years, back out there. But that's the kind of thing you don't really believe until you see it for yourself.

The funny thing is, I know logically I could take a holiday any time I wanted now. But I don't. Because I feel like I gave up my chance, and now I just have to wait until the end.

3:54:01

Today I was thinking about Barry a lot, which is unusual for me now. I suppose once, I used to— No. Stop it! That's phony. You don't *suppose* anything. You *know* you used to worry about him all the time. But that state of mind is so distant, so hard to identify with. I can only see things from where I am now. And from here, Barry doesn't matter at all.

4:01:49

Everything is changing faster and faster—as though suddenly my mind is catching up with my body. Was it only a few weeks ago that I wrote that entry about Barry not mattering? What made me think I was so superior to the person who was Barry's twin? What made me assume I will be immune to Barry's dominance—or that I could ever stop caring about him and what he thinks of me? But it was good to look at that entry again because it made me realize I'm going to have to be careful when I do go back out there—careful not to think I know everything. Will I really be ready to leave here in only two months?

4:12:13

Look at all the assumptions I made once about The Approaching One. Because of a distorted reflection of Its outward appearance, I was convinced It was monstrous, a destroyer and invader. (Barry was a lot more open-minded about it than I was now that I think about it. And I just assumed it was bravado on Barry's part.) Now, as The Approaching One nears the surface, I feel more of a bond with it than ever. But it's rational, not dreamy and romantic. Think of the sacrifice It is making, leaving Its own universe behind forever, leaving Its race behind, plunging alone into an unknown universe. I don't think evil creatures ever make sacrifices like that—at least I assume that's true.

But I can't make assumptions. I remember what I read last month about baby animals imprinting and those experiments with baby chimpanzees. An infant animal, separated from its mother, will start following the first thing that comes along, thinking *that* is its mother. In Africa, baby zebras have become passionately attached to jeeps. And in the experiments, the baby chimpanzees clung to their artificial wire mothers as though there were some comfort there—and later became psychotic.

Am I, separated from Barry, clinging in the same way to The Approaching One?

4:12:37

I woke up terrified today. It was awful, the loss of control. I haven't felt that way for so long, I forgot what it was like. It had nothing to do with Barry. I think it was what I wrote yesterday, about animals imprinting on mannikins and machines. What makes me think The Approaching One is not just a machine? It could be a robot, programmed to make this journey. In that case, It is sacrificing nothing. Its purpose could very well be evil. Am I deluding myself about It out of loneliness?

Later

But I'm not lonely. I'm peaceful and even happy here! And when I stand and watch The Approaching One, I'm not scared. I think what really terrified me was something else: leaving here and going back to that other world.

4:21:32

What I feel must be like stage fright. I've never been a performer, because I am terrified of being exposed in front of a crowd. I always have been. What's new is the other side, the *anticipation* of stepping out onstage. It wouldn't be thrilling if it wasn't chancy, if there wasn't something to be afraid of. That's how Barry must have felt all along. No wonder I disgusted him. I was constantly trying to drag him back, to cancel the show.

171

4:23:36

Less than a week. What would happen if I didn't go out? How soon would anybody—meaning Barry— notice? Probably not before 7:00, his time. That would be more than another year for me. What would happen in that year? Who would I be by then? Peaceful as it is, do I *want* to stay that much longer? And what about The Approaching One? Will It have come through by then? What would it be like to be in here with It when It *does* come through?

4:25:12

I look slowly over the different books, remembering what's in them, who I was and what I was feeling when I read them. It's something like saying good-bye to people I've met on a long ocean voyage, a cruise around the world. I've read about that experience, getting close to people and knowing you'll never see them again. But this is different, because the books will always be there whenever I want them. I'm the one who will be gone. Because I'll be somebody else.

4:25:36

Tomorrow I'll be a year older. I'm supposed to go out. And I'm scared. Because suddenly I know what going out will mean. It will be like pulling a fire alarm or like lighting a fuse. *Why didn't I see that until now?*

By stepping out that door, I will be setting free The Approaching One.

If I stay inside, it will be at least a year for me, perhaps several years, before It comes through. But out there, it will only be a matter of hours.

Why am I smiling? I once knew someone who used to smile when he was afraid. It baffled me then. Now I'm doing it. Who was that?

4:26:00

It was Barry, of course. I'm still smiling as I write this. I'm tingling all over. At the same time I feel calm, as The Approaching One is calm. I remember so many bad things, how imprisoned I was out there, how vulnerable and powerless. So easy to put it off, to delay seeing Barry, and the world. To delay the arrival of The Approaching One. The keys lie beside the notebook on the metal tabletop. I make my hand reach for them, grasp them. I stand up, still writing. I'm going out now.

20

When I stepped outside, the world did not look as I remembered it from six months and nine months ago. The light was different. It was not moonlight.

I walked slowly to the center of the meadow, filtering carefully, moderating the input so that my senses would not confuse me. I looked up. Somewhere out there beyond the stars lay the other universe, the singularity, and The Approaching One. And they were also twenty feet behind me, in the playhouse.

The stars were fading. I began to be aware of the wind in the leaves, the cold, stony babble of the river, the waking birds. My eyes rested on the horizon. A black line of trees against a red glow. I had forgotten about natural color. I had even forgotten about daylight. It had been a year of black and silver and gray.

I watched dark veils lifting away. The clouds were more colors than I had ever imagined, the earth so many different shades of green. I felt the vast expanse of prairie beneath my feet glide ponderously toward the sun. There was a pinpoint of fire, a hemisphere, an orange ball. At every instant the colors peaked, yet at every instant they grew more brilliant.

A rooster actually crowed. I laughed at the sheer corniness of it.

I watched until I could not look at the sun, and there was no longer any trace of rose in the sky. "And this happens every day out here," I said. And now my voice, a man's voice, did sound strange. It had been months since I had even talked to myself.

I shivered and looked at the calculator. It was 5:05 and galloping. With my thumb, I touched the off switch. The numbers that had been the terrible crux of my life for so long, my massive yoke—the numbers vanished. They didn't matter anymore.

Then I whooped and screamed, I cavorted, I pranced. I dashed to the river and plunged in. I could swim as long as I wanted. The numbers didn't matter anymore. I dove, I splashed, I shouted, I ran back to the meadow, I looked around at all the colors again, and the sun had dried me. I was hungry.

The house, as I approached it, seemed terribly unfamiliar. In my entire life I had only spent five days at this house, and that was a year ago. I passed slowly through the mounting room; I wandered around the kitchen I dimly remembered. And the events and details of the days I had spent here began to come back to me.

I opened and slammed cupboard doors, exclaiming in wonder at the amazing variety of food on the shelves and in the humming refrigerator. But I'd have to be careful what I ate for the first few days, or I'd make myself sick. A half cup of cornflakes would probably be safe, with a little milk, no fruit. I stared at the cereal box for some time. The idiotically grinning boy in the rainbow-colored photograph couldn't feel half as good as I did. I took the first bite slowly. The tender crisp texture, the rich taste were poetry. "You can have this every day," I told myself in the grown-up tones I couldn't get used to. I whooped again.

There was a creak of bedsprings upstairs, then footsteps. Barry

A fierce pang shot through me, a blossoming of bad memories. I grunted and stood up, knocking over the chair.

"Do you have to make so much damn noise, Harry? It's not even six thirty!" shouted a petulant, childish voice.

I picked up the chair and backed away from the table, suddenly remembering I was naked, fighting the impulse to run. Was I ready for this?

I stopped beside the window and the sink, facing the entrance to the hallway, from where Barry's voice was now coming.

"I know you got up so early to keep an eye on me, so you'd know if I tried to sneak outside. You're terrified of what I might do, aren't you, Harry. Do you *always* have to be so predictable?" Barry said, and came through the door.

He stopped. He was wearing the green running shorts I remembered from that day so long ago when Fred had died. His mouth was open, but whatever insult he was preparing ended as a guttural choke. He stared up at me, his sleepy eyes widening. "Huh?" he said in a startled voice.

He was much as I remembered him. But the calmness had not deserted me; it was there to draw upon, waiting to support me like a comfortable chair. "Don't you know me, Barry?" I said, looking down into his eyes, beginning to smile.

"Know you?" He was confused. Then he wailed. "Harry! Harry, no!" He squeezed his eyes shut and shook his head violently. He opened them again and stared at me, "*Harry!*" he moaned.

He had never, even in our closest days, exposed so much emotion to me, so much vulnerability. My heart opened up to him. And suddenly I needed him. I ran forward and hugged him. The top of his head came to my ear. "Barry. Don't, Barry. It's still me," I soothed, rocking him.

He broke away roughly. His eyes were full of tears. "I don't believe . . . But it *is* you! Oh, my God." Red-faced, he ran for the stairs.

I followed him. I heard his bedroom door slam as I reached the second floor. I passed the bathroom. I remembered that there was a full-length mirror inside this bathroom door. I went into the bathroom, closed the door and looked at myself in the mirror for the first time in a year.

A tall stranger looked back at me.

His face was long, the chin and jawline sharp-edged. My cheeks had been round; he had cheekbones, emphasized by the dark shadow of beard—

though I thought I had shaved carefully that morning. Muscles jutted from his chest and rippled horizontally across his belly, so sharply etched they might have been outlined in black ink. I could see veins branching across his forearms and on the backs of his hands. And where had that nose come from? Maybe it was a little *too* long. I looked at his profile and decided I liked it fine. From this angle I could see the dark, tightly woven braid that hung down his neck. It added a pleasing touch of femininity. He reminded me of the archetypical Indian brave.

I peered into his eyes. The way they watched me also made me think of an Indian. The eyes were the most unfamiliar part of him, placid, steady, unguarded—with maybe just a hint of the demonic around the edges.

The Indian youth swung away. A blond, sulky boy stood in the doorway. He looked athletic, as I remembered. But now, compared to the older boy in the mirror, his head seemed a little too large for his shoulders, his limbs even a trifle scrawny.

"How . . . how long were you in there?" Barry said, in his high-pitched, still changing voice. He seemed hesitant.

"From one thirty to four twenty-six—with two fifteen-minute breaks."

"So that was . . ." He bit his lip, trying to calculate. Then he frowned. A lot of things were coming back to me, and I remembered that expression. It meant frustration. He was having trouble calculating. In a minute he'd stamp his foot and demand the answer.

But instead he looked down at the floor and pouted, his hands clasped behind his back. His eyes darted up to my face and then quickly away.

He was shy. He was even a little afraid of me! He didn't dare get angry yet or demand anything from me at all.

"A year," I told him.

"You were in there a year?" He looked directly up at me now, bewildered. "How...how could you stand it?"

"I did it, that's all. It was good."

"Good? But that's crazy... How come you talk so funny, act so funny?" he said. It was another old trick, avoiding the issue by going on the offensive. "Your voice sounds so...dead, kind of. Your face...You don't make any expressions."

"I got out of the habit, I guess, not talking to anyone for a year."

My calmness seemed to infuriate him. And now that the initial shock was over, his anger was getting the better of his timidity. "Well, *I* never would have done that crazy thing. But you were so *scared* I would that you did it yourself. Because you believed me. Only I was lying." He threw the words at me like a taunt, a dare. "Funny, isn't it. You went through that whole year for nothing."

I watched him. "No," I said. "At the beginning, I went in because I was frightened. But for nothing?" I laughed a little, just to give him some kind of expression. "No, Barry. It was the most important thing I ever did. I wouldn't take back any of it. And if you made me do it, then all I can say is—thanks."

179

"Thanks? You're *thanking* me for driving you to do that? You *are* crazy. You were crazy when you went in, and you're crazier now."

He glared at me, waiting for some kind of response. But I had nothing to say. If the way I felt now was crazy, then crazy was wonderful. I smiled. "Is this the kind of expression you would like?" I asked.

He clenched his fists and howled. "You're *crazy!*" he said, for the fourth time. (Had he always had such a limited vocabulary?) "And don't act so . . . so holier-than-thou about it. You were afraid, that's all, so you ran away and hid out in there. And now you're trying to make it seem like it was something wonderful that you did. But you were really just too scared and weak to do anything else."

"You're wrong, Barry!" I said. He was knocking the calmness right out from under me. "You don't think it was scary, what I did? You don't think it was hard? That isn't fair! You didn't do it!"

"'That isn't fair,'" he mimicked me, just like in the old days.

"Don't talk to me like that!" I shouted, and stepped forward.

Something changed in his face. His eyes wavered and slid away from me. His head bent to the side. He never would have done *that* in the old days. Was it because of what I had just said, asserting myself as I had never done before? Or was it just because he was afraid I would hit him?

"Oh, Barry, why are we doing this?" I said. I did feel scared now—scared of what *I* might do if I lost my calmness and control. To be physically threatening was the last thing I had ever intended. I practiced my smile. "It's great seeing you again, Barry. I mean it. I really missed you."

Gently, I put my hand on his shoulder. I wasn't sure it was the right gesture, but I did want to touch him somehow. And I really was glad to see him, despite his bullying, and the bad memories and fears it brought back. I loved him. I cared about him more than anyone else.

Still, I might not have been *quite* as glad to see him if I hadn't been three inches taller and a year older than he was.

I caught a glimpse of my face in the mirror. How smug I looked! I hastily corrected my expression.

"But you aren't even... I mean..." Barry looked down at the large hand on his shoulder and then up into my face. "Great seeing me again, huh? Well, seeing *you* isn't like seeing Harry again. Harry's gone. I'll never see him again." His voice teetered on the edge of hysteria. He squirmed away from my hand as though he was still afraid I might hurt him. "You took my brother away! I can't have him back. You killed him! It's just the same as if you killed him!"

Now I was confused. Barry wasn't just angry. He was grieving. He was acting like a bereaved person.

Could I have been wrong about him? Maybe he *hadn't* wanted to get rid of me. Maybe he had never really hated being a twin at all.

"But... but wait a minute," I said. "I thought... I thought you—"

"You thought wrong!" he screamed at me, tears in his eyes.

The mirror shivered. Downstairs, dirty dishes clattered in the sink.

"Wow!" I said. "What a funny feeling! But... but it's kind of familiar too."

Barry seemed a lot more unnerved by the little tremor than I was; his face had gone dead white. "You don't know what that was?"

"It wasn't an earthquake?"

He shook his head at me. "No."

"What is it, Barry? Tell me."

"The creature in the playhouse. It just came through."

21

The Approaching One. It had been my companion in the playhouse for a year—though I had never seen anything but its reflection. And now, it seemed, we were going to meet face to face at last.

"Come on," I said. I looked back at Barry from the top of the stairs. He was still standing in the bathroom doorway. "I think I left the keys on the kitchen table."

He moved forward reluctantly, watching me. What was the matter with him now? The way he was creeping toward me reminded me of a rabbit. I had the feeling that if I suddenly said "Boo!" he'd turn and scamper away. Why did I remember him as being so easygoing? He certainly seemed to have changed in the year I'd been gone.

No. That wasn't it. Nothing had happened to Barry. He'd just been asleep all night. It was me who had changed. That was why I saw him differently. How long would it take me to get used to it?

"It's exciting," I said as we went down the stairs.

"I've been thinking a lot about the event horizon and the singularity. Now we're going to find out some things."

"You aren't . . . afraid?" he asked me in the kitchen.

I picked up the keys and looked at them in my hand. "Afraid? A little bit, I guess." I shrugged. "But that doesn't make any difference. Nobody can stop It now."

"How do you know?"

"Huh?" He looked so pale and unsure, standing there on the rag rug. "I was in there a long time, watching It," I said. "I thought a lot. I . . . began to understand things. I felt a lot of Its energy. Sometimes I even thought It was communicating with me. And It can't be stopped whether we're afraid or not. That's all."

"Communicating with you?" Barry sounded more suspicious than ever. "Or doing something to your head? Changing the way you see it, so you wouldn't try to stop it from coming through or try to stop the invasion?"

"I thought about that too. But it doesn't make any difference now. And it's not the way you think. . . Barry! *You're* afraid!" I was confused again. "But before. . . you were the one who didn't want me to warn anybody about it."

He looked away from me. "Yeah, I know. But I didn't think it would be so soon. And before this. . . this happened to you, I didn't really know how powerful that place was. Even though you told me. It was more like a kind of game. It seems a lot bigger now. I never thought it would happen like this."

"Funny how things happen," I said. "Six months ago I ran into a cop, out on the road. It must have been, oh, around 3:00 A.M., your time. I never even thought of telling him."

"You didn't?" He looked wistfully at the phone. "It still might not be too late."

"It's too late. Come on, let's go see." I slung my arm over his shoulder and propelled him gently but firmly out of the room, away from the phone. He didn't try to resist. It was obvious that I was much stronger.

"I just can't get over the sky, and the sun," I said, out in the blazing raucous meadow. "It was almost worth living without them for a year to learn how much of a miracle they really are."

Barry looked away from me, embarrassed. I probably did sound sappy. It would take me a while to learn how to behave around other people.

"Don't worry, Barry, you can trust me," I said, squeezing his shoulder.

"I know what that creature looks like," he said. "It looks like it was meant to kill. And if it was communicating with you, that's even worse. It changed you, so you wouldn't try to stop it."

I felt a flicker of doubt. Could he possibly be right? Quickly, I pushed the doubt away. I had a year's more experience with The Approaching One than he did. I knew how important this arrival was. Having other people around would ruin it. It was pretty generous of me to include Barry—he hadn't earned it, the way I had. I lifted my arm from his shoulder. "You don't have to come if you'd rather not," I told him.

185

"If you go, I go," he said, and marched ahead of me into the circle of trees.

He was scared, but he wouldn't let me go alone. I remembered the night he had dragged me with him to the playhouse, the first we had heard something come through. Maybe he had been scared then too, and had needed me to help him be brave. Maybe he had always needed me.

A girl was standing inside the trees. She started to greet Barry. Then she saw me. "Who's he?" she quickly mouthed at Barry. I stepped past the sundial, and she blushed and looked away.

"Lucy!" I said. I was surprised at how glad I felt to see her. "Don't you remember me?"

"Remember you?"

"It's Harry," Barry told her.

"Harry?" she said, making a questioning face at Barry. Then she gasped and put her hand over her mouth. She shook her head, her eyes wide above her hand.

"What's the matter, Lucy?" I said.

She didn't take her hand away or stop shaking her head. Her eyes kept getting wider, her face pinker, as she stared at me.

Then I saw what at least part of the problem was. "Oh," I said, blushing a little myself. "I forgot all about clothes. They're inside." I stepped toward the door.

A shrieking wail like a demented siren came tearing from inside the playhouse. There was a thud, and a shudder as a two-foot round dent bulged out of the thick steel wall.

"I . . . I think you better wait until later to get your clothes," Lucy said, backing away.

22

Barry and Lucy huddled against one another, their hands over their ears, as the high-pitched screams continued. I looked at them, and was reminded of a terrible emotion I had forgotten about.

I stepped to the door and put the key in the lock.

"What are you doing?" Barry howled.

"It needs to get out," I explained, raising my voice against the shrieks and the noisy battering. "It'll knock the place down if I don't open the door."

"No! Don't!" Barry bellowed. But he didn't try to stop me. "He's crazy, he went nuts in there!" he babbled to Lucy as I turned the keys in the shuddering door. "That thing did something to him, made him a slave. It's controlling his mind!"

I pushed open the door and got out of the way.

Out reared the head, swinging back and forth—though it wasn't really a head, only a pair of metallic jaws about the size of a small stepladder. Laserlike red points gleamed from the ends of the black conical teeth. Behind the hinge, the jaws were attached to a snakelike body of interlocked cylinders the color of steel, about a foot in diameter where they joined the head. Whiplike, convulsive, the thing uncoiled from the door, the jaws pointed skyward, darting and circling. As It emerged, we could see that the body grew narrower, diminishing to a needlelike point at the end.

We were outside the circle of trees now, peering at It past the sundial. It spasmed and thrashed on the long meadow grasses, glinting in the sunlight, wailing like some terrible fire alarm.

Until the jaws managed to catch the lashing tail and clamp down upon it. The shrieking stopped instantly. Its echo vanished in our ears as we watched the jaws hungrily gobble the needlelike point, and then more. The teeth crunched down on the thickening cylinders like a crocodile devouring an eel. Only the eel was the end of Its own body.

It was a bright circle on the grass, diminishing rapidly. The jaws continued their busy work, ravenous, gulping. The circle shrank. And then It was an oval, the length of the snapping jaws. The jaws began to bend, metallic but pliable. The neck was gone. The jaws curved around and enveloped the hinge. Now It was the size of an inner tube, the jaws no longer snapping but inching forward upon themselves, bent double and still bending. The inner tube contracted. It was a silvery beach ball, dwindling. A basketball, a tennis ball, a golf ball, a marble, a bright spot of light.

And then nothing.

We stared down at the empty patch of grass. It had

happened so quickly. The thing had emerged, devoured itself and was gone—and I could still feel my eardrums vibrating from its cries. There was something appalling about the efficiency with which It had self-destructed.

There had not been enough room to do the job inside the playhouse. If I had not let It out—and I wasn't sure what had made me do it—It would have battered the walls to pieces in Its rage to get out and destroy itself.

"Years and years in the event horizon," I said. "And then It comes through and . . . and just eats itself up."

"It's crazy," Barry said. "Meaningless, and stupid, and . . . crazy!"

"*I'm* going crazy!" Lucy said. "I can't hardly believe it even happened. It did happen, didn't it?"

"It happened," I said. "Maybe there'll be some answers inside." I hurried back into the circle of trees.

"Aren't you coming, Barry?" I heard Lucy ask him just behind me.

"But what if there's something else . . . ? Sure, I'm coming," he said angrily.

I propped open the door. A lot of the metal furniture was twisted and scattered around the room. Pages from books drifted everywhere. But what was really startling was the floor. The granite slab was split down the middle, the two separated halves as cracked and fissured as the windshield of a wrecked car.

"What happened?" Barry said.

"We'll find out," I said. It was a little saddening to see my home demolished. Fortunately my diary, which had been pushed under the bed, was unharmed. I stood up with the notebook in my hand.

"Listen. Outside," Lucy said, turning toward the door.

There were sirens, real ones this time, and car doors slamming, and voices.

"They must have heard all the noise," Barry said. He sounded relieved. "Now they're coming to see what happened."

"But that's wrong," I said, and I remembered what it felt like to be truly afraid.

"*What's* wrong?" Barry demanded.

"Just look out there!"

In the rectangle of the doorway, the meadow grasses trembled delicately in the hot breeze. A red bird fluttered down to land on the sundial. The voices were getting closer, though we could still hear the sounds of the river.

"I don't see anything," Barry said as though he thought I'd meant another monster.

"The world's alive out there! It's not frozen. Time's the same in here now." I felt dizzy.

"It's *normal*," Lucy said.

"But . . . " I was thinking as hard and fast as I ever had in my life. "Wait a minute . . . I think maybe I get it," I said slowly, sitting down on the wrecked bed.

"Get what?" Barry said.

He knew my mind was racing far ahead of his, and he hated it. I could hear it in the tone of his voice. In a minute he'd be furious at me. To avoid having a fight, I had to explain what had happened in a way that wouldn't make him angry.

Then I caught myself. It was the old pattern again—even his tone of voice was a way of controlling me. But why shouldn't I know more about the playhouse? I was the one who had lived here. And what was so terrible about having an argument?

But there wasn't time to explain much now. I pushed open the trapdoor and hoisted myself through.

"What are you doing?" Lucy asked me.

"We're on real time now. Mustn't forget. This place is just like the rest of the world. Which means those people will be here any second." I grinned down through the opening. "So I better find some pants that fit me—real quick."

◻

23

The first thing the police did was to make sure nobody was hurt. Then they wanted to know what we had done to set off the explosion that had cracked the granite slab and triggered the siren that had brought them here.

Before, Barry had wanted to keep the place a secret so that the cops wouldn't come and take the adventure away from us. But now that they had found out about it, he saw no reason not to tell them everything. He enjoyed the attention and the chance to come across as an authority.

I wasn't sure how much I wanted to tell. But it would have been cruel to let Barry look like a fool in front of them. So I went along with his explanations and backed up everything he said.

They thought we were hysterical.

They knew the property had a bad reputation. Apparently we had set off some kind of explosive device the old man had built into the place. Naturally we would be scared and a little confused. But why did we insist on making up these crazy stories?

Barry began to be really upset. But the more he insisted, the less they believed him. Especially when he kept trying to convince them that we were twins. The irony of it was horribly frustrating for him. He had always seemed to hate it when people made a fuss about our being twins. But now that it was vital for them to recognize it, they wouldn't.

Or maybe, it occurred to me, he really *hadn't* minded people noticing our resemblance as much as I had thought. Maybe that had been another misinterpretation on my part.

The argument dragged on and on. Lucy, who had been through the same disorienting experience, had no more credibility than we had. So finally I said, "We aren't saying another word until we talk to our lawyer, Mr. Crane."

"Lawyer?" Barry said.

"Why do you need a lawyer?" one of the cops said. "We're not pressing charges now."

"Just ask Mr. Crane about the Krasner boys and if they're twins or not," I said. "And we're not saying anything else. Our story's too valuable to leak out one more word without his advice—whether you believe it or not. Isn't that right, Barry?"

"Huh?...Oh...That's right, Harry," Barry said. A grin spread slowly across his face. He was finally beginning to realize what the lawyer would tell them about our being twins.

They roped off the playhouse and set up a guard around it, just as Barry had predicted they would. They made sure that there were no other explosive devices on the property. Two police cars and a couple of officers stayed to keep watch by the playhouse.

The others came inside. We phoned Mr. Crane, but his secretary said he was away for the day and would get back to us tomorrow. We told the cops he would call them, and soon after that they left.

It was a little disappointing. Barry, even more than I, had been looking forward to Mr. Crane's conversation with the police. But we were beginning to relax a bit. "I can't believe you talked to the cops that way," Barry said, looking at me with amusement and with another expression that almost might have been pride. He didn't need to add that the old Harry never would have done anything like that.

Now Barry and Lucy wanted to know what I thought had happened back at the playhouse. Barry didn't seem to mind too much that I might know more about it than he did. We sat down at the kitchen table.

"It plugged up the singularity somehow, closed it off, maybe it even ate it, I don't know," I said. "But that's what Its function had to be. It came through, stopped the singularity and then self-destructed."

"But why?" Barry said. "Why close up something so important, a hole into another universe? Why not study it, explore what's on the other side?"

I shrugged. "I guess they didn't see it that way over there. Maybe to them the singularity was dangerous, or a nuisance—sucking things out of their universe into ours. Maybe it could have done a lot of damage. Maybe the creature was even *protecting* us, closing off an entrance that made us vulnerable. It looked horrible, but . . . I think It was benevolent." I closed my eyes for a moment, remembering all the time I had spent alone with The Approaching One. "It did a good deed, I'm sure of that. It saved us, maybe from something really terrible that could have gotten through . . . Though I guess a robot can't really sacrifice itself."

"How do you know it was a robot and not a creature?" Lucy said. She couldn't take her eyes off me. It made me a little embarrassed. She seemed to think I was some kind of authority, a wise and intriguing stranger. But she also seemed a little frightened, as Barry had been.

"I don't know. But in some ways a robot would make sense. It wouldn't care about leaving home forever, going on a one-way trip to another universe. A robot could be programmed to self-destruct when the job was done, so it would have as little effect on this side as possible. I don't know. I have to think about it. If It *wasn't* a robot, if It did all that willingly, to save us . . . then It's the most magnificent creature I ever heard of."

"That thing? To eat itself up like that? Ugh!" Lucy said. "It makes me feel sick." She stood up. "Time for lunch. I better eat at home today."

Barry walked her out. It was something of a relief to see them go. I had been feeling edgy, and now I knew why. I did my one hundred push-ups and three hundred sit-ups, and felt a lot better. Barry was still gone, and I figured he was eating at Lucy's. I had something to eat myself and then cleaned up the prodigious mess of dirty dishes around the sink. I hunted through Uncle Ambrose's closets and found some clothes that fit me better than my skimpy ones. He even had an old baggy pair of shorts which I wore when I went running for a couple of hours in the late afternoon. It was a whole new experience for me to run and see my location change with every step. I hadn't begun to get used to how beautiful everything was.

I meditated up in my little bedroom. It wasn't successful. I was still so keyed up about his new world that I couldn't really lose myself. So I cooked supper. That was fun.

Neither Barry nor I ate very much. We talked a lot, mostly about Mom and Dad, and what would be the best way to help them deal with the situation. "Well, at least Mom won't have trouble telling us apart anymore," Barry said at one point.

"You know she could always tell us apart, even before you got her to stop making us wear the same clothes," I said.

"What are you talking about?" Barry seemed surprised. "She was always making mistakes."

"She was just kidding around," I said. "She even told me once."

"She was just kidding?"

"Of course. You mean you really didn't know that?"

"But..." Then Barry scowled. "Sure, I knew. Don't be such a jerk. *I* was just kidding. And you fell for it, as usual."

My first inclination was to drop the subject, so that he wouldn't get any angrier. He didn't want to admit that he had been wrong, and I was letting him get away with it. But why should I? "Why do you have to be so mean, Barry?" I asked him. "And why do you have to lie? So what if you were wrong about that one thing? I've been wrong about a lot of things. Everybody is. I think I was wrong about you a lot of the time."

He looked away from me. "Okay, okay, I'm sorry. Maybe I *was* wrong," he admitted, and changed the subject.

We fought about the dishes. He wanted to leave them. I wanted to get them done—and I wanted him to help, after all the cleaning up I'd done that afternoon. "How are you going to make me?" he demanded. "You going to beat me up?" And he slammed out the back door.

I tried not to resent him, but I couldn't help it. I was angry. Why should I clean up after him? But if I just left them, then I'd be doing what he wanted. There was nothing to do but persist and wash them myself. I kept making myself remember The Approaching One in the event horizon, imperturbable and calm. It helped, a little. What helped a lot was when Barry came back inside, five minutes later, and picked up the dish towel and began drying.

I didn't say anything. But I felt a little bit like crying. I hadn't done anything to make him give in. He had done it on his own. It was as though he was admitting that he liked the way I am now. And maybe he had always liked me more than I ever realized. Maybe both of us had been mistaken about a lot of things, and had never known it until now.

We were both tired and went up to our rooms

after we finished the dishes. I sat down to write in my diary. I had so much to say that I was worried at first about how I could cram it all into one-half page. Then I remembered—I could have all the pages I wanted.

That kind of thing keeps happening again and again. Suddenly I realize some little detail of what it's like out here that I'd forgotten about—and usually it's something wonderful.

One thing that isn't so wonderful is the problem of Mom and Dad. I feel a little guilty about what my change might do to them and keep wondering how to explain it. Once they get over the initial shock, I hope they'll be all right. If Barry can adjust to me, then they should be able to. I'll find out soon enough. They'll be here a week from tomorrow.

And a week is really no time at all.

ABOUT THE AUTHOR

WILLIAM SLEATOR graduated from Harvard with a degree in English and spent a year in England studying musical composition and working as a pianist. For nine years he was a rehearsal pianist for the Boston Ballet and composed three ballets for that company. He now lives in Boston and devotes himself to writing full-time. William Sleator's other popular novels for young adults include, *Fingers*, *Interstellar Pig*, *The Boy Who Reversed Himself*, and *The Duplicate*.